the court of
m e d b

This is a work of fiction. Names, characters, organizations, businesses, places, events and incidents either are the product of the author's imagination or are used fictitiously. Any resemblance to actual persons, living or dead, or actual events is entirely coincidental.

Published by Snowy Wings Publishing
Turner, Oregon
www.snowywingspublishing.com

Cover designed by Regina Wamba of MaeIDesign.com.
Interior by Key of Heart Designs.
Interior graphics designed by Dover Publications, Inc.

ISBN: 978-1-952667-65-7

praise for annie cosby

the court of medb

SOULS OUT OF IRELAND, BOOK TWO

annie cosby

Snowy Wings PUBLISHING

pronunciation guide

Abeg: *ah-BEG*

Ailill: *AH-leel*

Badb: *baiv*

Bríd: *breej*

Cruachan: *CRU-uh-khan*

Faolan: *FWALE-on*

Findabair: *FINN-uh-var*

Leanbh: *LAHN-uv*

Maine: *MA-nuh*

Medb: *mayve*

Moira: *MOY-ruh*

Morrigu: *mor-ig-OO*

Ollam: *OH-lav*

Ríona: *REE-uh-nuh*

In the Irish language, like in any language, spellings and pronunciations have changed over the centuries, and dialects still differ from region to region. Throughout the Souls Out of Ireland series, I've tried to be consistent in the spelling of each individual name or word. In most places where there was a choice to be made, I've used the older, Irish spellings (like "Medb" instead of "Maeve"). Sometimes the choice wasn't so clear-cut, or I simply chose wrong, so I apologize for any place this isn't consistent.

A big thank you to my translator, Rebecca, who translated the Irish parts of the novel. As usual, any mistakes were mine alone.

"That crazed girl improvising her music.

Her poetry, dancing upon the shore,

Her soul in division from itself . . ."

—william butler yeats

daoine á thiach
THE HUNTED

m o i r a

Every sound, every crunch of leaves, every whisper of the wind was a threat. My body vibrated with fear. Fear for me, for my sisters, for our father, for these boys who had found themselves tangled up in our plight. I felt like a fraud riding Bó while my sisters trudged along through the undergrowth of the forest unprotected. And I did feel protected. Not just because of what Louis had called Bó—the *fíorláir*, the True Mare. *Lucky, blessed, safe from witchcraft or enchantment, as is her rider.* That was what Louis had said. I didn't know if I believed it, but I did know that I felt protected when I rode Bó and that wasn't new. I'd always felt that way.

Her mane brushed against my hands, and I rubbed her gray flank. At the average size for a Connemara pony, Bó was a bit small for me and Aidan both to ride comfortably, and she had acted quite unreasonable at being asked to do so. But she'd soon warmed to Aidan,

our erstwhile houseguest, who was quite helpless at the moment, and now she and I both drew strength and comfort from him. He was an uneasy rider and kept his hands tight around my stomach. The injury to his midriff from the kelpie attack back at home was nearly healed, but now a long gash traced the length of his lower leg, from the fighting on the rustyback hill. He couldn't move very fast on his own, and I could tell he was in great pain because he bit down every time Bó swayed or made a tiny leap over a fallen log.

As we rode, Bríd's confession back at the ruins of our castle was on my mind: the dreams she'd been having about my death—and that it wasn't the first dream she'd had foretelling a death. She'd seen our mother die in childbirth, our new little sibling gone too soon, before it had come to pass. For that reason, she didn't think the things that came to her while she slept were dreams at all. She thought they were premonitions. My heart twinged with the memory of our mother at the stream within the woods at home. No, it wasn't our mother. Even though she felt so real and called us by the pet names our mother had borrowed from her mother's tongue, Yoruba—*Taiwo*, *Kehinde*, and *Eta Oko*. Even so. That was just a shade. A *bean nighe*. A bit of magic.

Still, I would have given anything to turn and ride straight back to that shade. To the image of our mother. To the rustyback hill and the ruins of Bunrowan Castle.

But we couldn't go back. That much was clear. Whoever was chasing us would always find us on the rustyback.

Bríd walked close to Bó's side, as if afraid to let me get very far. She spoke little, and I could see the guilt in her downcast eyes. She'd looked paler than usual since we left, her skin nearly matching mine for the first time in our lives, though nothing else about our features would have people thinking us sisters. We may not have known our biological families, but we knew Bríd's genes weren't all Celt. Kids at home used to tease that her real family was the Chinese family in Clifden. The little boy in that family even approached Bríd on a playground once to ask if she was Chinese too. Bríd had simply said that she was Irish and walked away, an uncharacteristic slump to her shoulders. A similar slump was evident beneath the bulky sweater she wore now. The wool was singed with the marks of battle, and her black hair hung limply past her shoulders. It was nowhere near as disheveled as my own red bob, which I tucked behind my ears, but for Bríd, it was bad. My normally vivacious, stunning sister looked like a shadow of herself.

Every so often, her hand crept out and glided along Bó's flank. Annoyance flared in my stomach. Bríd thought she had premonitions in her sleep, and she'd kept that from me and Ríona. For how many years? And then she'd lied to the *bean nighe* to keep her secret, causing the destruction of our home. The castle was in ruins. What else had she lied about? Kept from us? What did she keep from us still?

And how in God's name could I protect my sisters when they had secrets like this?

Bríd's shoulders sagged as she walked, and sometimes stumbled, through the brush that Bó easily crushed beneath her feet. Bríd looked tired, dispirited, beat. Guilty. So very unlike Bríd. Fear flickered through my gut yet again. The need to protect my sisters ran through my veins like blood, but now it was me they worried for.

And it wasn't just Bríd's premonition. Ríona and Louis had witnessed the omen too. These mysterious boys had turned up and started hanging around our home just in time for some serious trouble. Like Bó crying tears of blood. The Blood Omen, Louis had called it. The blood tears of a mare were supposed to foretell the death of her rider, and Louis had professed he hadn't seen the omen in a century.

I looked at his lean back as he led the way through this dark forest near the coast, Ríona at his side, her wolf, Faolan, at hers. Ríona turned to me, as if she could feel my gaze. Her curls were tied into a thick ponytail with an old yellow satin scarf of Mam's, holding it away from her brown forehead and warm eyes. She gave me a small, reassuring smile, trusting where I could not. Ríona hadn't spoken a word in her life. With perfect hearing and sight, her inability or unwillingness to speak had caused many to say mean things over the years. But what they didn't understand is that Ríona understood people better than anyone I knew.

Again, I looked at Louis. He was the only one of us who knew this land like the back of his hand. And so, he led us toward Ros a' Mhil, where we would look for passage to the Aran Islands. At least that's what he said. Could we really trust him?

We had little choice. When he'd insisted that I ride the True Mare for protection, I hadn't resisted, even though the others had to walk. Could Bó protect me from premonition and omen and whatever else was headed our way? I didn't know. But I wanted to believe.

Because if I couldn't be protected, if I didn't endure to protect my sisters . . . who would?

Bríd's crow, Finbar, flew on ahead of us, his keen eyes scouting for danger, occasionally circling back around behind us to check that we weren't being followed. The men we'd fought on the rustyback hill may have fled or perished, but I believed that one vile man's last words: that many hundreds were after us now. Hunting us. Like prey.

And all those hunters believed the blood of the Morrigan ran through our veins. That Ríona was something called the Morrigu. They had been promised a mysterious crown in return for the delivery of my sister into the hands of an evil queen.

coimirce aistir

SAFE PASSAGE

ríona

The dark surrounds. It sidles up beside you, quiet as a whisper, and when you finally realize something is there and look up, you're lost in it. Darkness. Only the flickering auras of your friends for company. At least, that's how it is when you're being chased across a country you don't know nearly as well as you thought you did.

I walked beside Louis, his tall, lean frame striding confidently through the dark, only a sliver of moonlight shining on his auburn hair and making his white skin even paler. He bravely led our little band of warriors over fallen branches and under dense canopies growing between tightly packed trees. My chest pounded with my companions' confused energies, not to mention a strange fear I was fairly sure would become a familiar friend before long.

Between Bríd's confession of deathly premonitions and the dead man's confession on the rustyback hill, it seemed I had much to fear.

Why did this evil Queen Medb want me? What crown had she promised to the hordes chasing us? And was I, Ríona Doyle, truly the Morrigu? I didn't feel like it. I felt like Ríona Doyle.

But even the *bean nighe*, the spirit that looked so like our mother, had said it: *The Morrigan runs through your veins.*

Not to mention the old woman who'd shown up on our doorstep, ranting about a frenzy and a great queen. She'd called *me* "great queen." She'd said I had the frenzy in me. Of course, I was less inclined to believe a threatening stranger than our own mother, even if I knew in my heart that the *bean nighe* wasn't our mother.

None of this makes any sense.

My fingers ruffled Faolan's shaggy red fur as he loped along beside me on his gangly legs. His golden eyes forever roved the shadows around us, his long nose and sharp ears on high alert.

There was a soft vibration deep within me, as if something were dormant, lying there in wait. Whatever it was, it had come alive back on the rustyback hill.

The ghost of a deep buzz whispered across my skin; it felt like the memory of the bees that had swarmed at my will in the battle at the castle. Had I really controlled them, or had it been coincidence? If it had been me, my own sheer will, where had that power come from? Louis had said it was us—me and my sisters—who were making the curios back at our castle. But it wasn't like I hadn't tried such things before. Just days ago, I'd holed up in my room and tried to manipulate a curio. It hadn't worked then, when I'd been focused and trying, so why would it have worked when I'd been desperate and confused and fighting for my life?

I was afraid to give room in my mind to the biggest question of all, but it kept returning, nudging at me, growing bigger, stronger, more prominent.

Did this *power* have something to do with the Morrigu?

I couldn't believe it was possible. At least, I couldn't admit to myself that I believed it possible. Even though I did.

Faolan gave a grumble and I followed his gaze to Louis's stout brown hound, Conry, who trotted obediently at Louis's heels.

You best get used to him, I admonished Faolan silently. He only grumbled more loudly. I stole a glance at Louis. He never seemed to tire, walking onward with the determination of a warrior. The large sword he'd wielded back at the castle had disappeared. I didn't know what he'd done with it, but he looked no less confident in its absence.

There were so many questions that needed answering, yet on we marched without daring to ask any of them. I glanced at the tattoo on Louis's arm. The triskele. I trusted Louis. I did. Despite everything. And still the sight of the swirling mark made indelible on his skin sent a frisson of fear through me. What had he sworn to protect? To hide from us?

I didn't ask again. Not yet. When we reached our destination, there would be time enough for catching our breath, finding a way around the triskele oath, and demanding answers. For the time being, Louis was the only one of us who knew his way across Ireland, how to truly navigate the craggy hills of Galway. After all, we'd lived in relative isolation at Bunrowan Castle all our lives, and Aidan . . . well. Aidan had apparently lived beneath the sea for the past decade. It was down to Louis to keep us moving toward Ros a' Mhil, a town in Connemara where he and Aidan had agreed we'd best be able to find a way to Inis Mór.

And there, if we were lucky, we would find an ally.

I looked at Aidan, whose big brown eyes were as round and dark as ever below his messy mop of brown hair. With one arm around Moira, Aidan rubbed his forehead with the back of his other hand, his signature nervous tell. He was fairly sure we would find his father on Inis Mór, the largest of the Aran Islands off the west coast of Galway. And he was certain if anyone in this country would help us, *could* help us, it was his father, who he said "knew about these things." Whatever that meant. Louis agreed it was the best move we could make now, because nobody in pursuit of us would expect it. Moira, Bríd, and I had no ties to the Aran Islands, and Inis Mór was in the very opposite direction of Dublin or any of the other large cities, where it would no doubt be expected we'd go to look for our dad.

With the sanctuary the island afforded, and the help of Aidan's father, we would finally devise a strategy to find Dad without being caught by the people hunting us. The people hunting *me*.

bricfeasta

BREAKFAST

bríd

Ros a' Mhil arose within sight just before dawn on our first day without a home. Without our home. It had all been my doing. It was all my fault.

The guilt solidified in my stomach like a stone. I feared this stone was a permanent addition to the landscape of my body, my being. Who I was and who I would forever be.

"We should set up camp," Louis said, his slight English accent picking out the word *camp*. He signaled for Conry to stop, and they both turned back, as we'd finally reached the end of the interminable woods.

"Just when we're about to get out of these feckin' woods?" I grumbled, stretching my legs as Bó came to a halt beside me.

"Let's hunker down here before it gets light out," Louis went on, ignoring me. "So we can keep you out of sight and not draw any

attention to ourselves while we figure out our next steps."

Moira slid off Bó and then turned to help Aidan down. He grimaced in pain. Ríona sat in front of a nearby ash tree and leaned back, stretching her arms above her head. Faolan curled at her side and gave a great yawn. I looked to the sky for Finbar, but he was nowhere to be seen. Wind swirled in my veins, twirling my wrists, as if my very blood was begging for freedom. Finbar had been doing great circles around us all night. Hopefully, he was still doing his rounds. We needed his sight now more than ever.

"So, what are we going to do?" Aidan asked, as Moira helped him off of Bó. He landed on the ground with an uncomfortable thump. "We don't know the schedule for the public ferry."

I kept my eyes on the ground. Despite the guilt threatening to swallow me, I still had room to feel annoyance with Aidan. It was all I could do not to scream when I saw him, in my dreams, leaving my poor, helpless sister to die on a pebbled beach.

But that was just a dream. A dream eerily like the one I'd had shortly before our mother died. Premonition. Dream. Prophecy. The word didn't matter. All that mattered was that it didn't come true. And I could only guarantee that by keeping Moira away from Aidan.

"We can't take the ferry," Louis said, shaking his head. Despite it being his idea to "hunker down" here, he was the only one who hadn't yet taken a seat. Even Conry walked to the edge of the woods and sat there, facing away from us, his spine straight, his ears perked. "Too risky, with all the tourists and locals. Anyone could be on a boat like that. The last thing we need is to be ambushed in open water."

"Then how exactly are we going to get there, pray tell?" Moira asked with a tight smile. "Swim?"

Louis crossed his arms. "You and your selkie there are welcome to do that, if you'd like. But I was going to propose we find a private boat for hire."

Aidan and Moira exchanged a look. Aidan gave her a nonchalant shrug, but Moira's nerves were clearly frayed. And I was fairly sure Louis would be the one to bear the brunt of her ire. I didn't think I could handle a squabble now, not with the guilt hanging so heavily upon me. I'd added so much to Moira's worries, and Ríona's, and everyone's.

"How do we find one of those?" I piped up, hoping to forestall any arguments.

"Well," Louis said, sighing, "it's a fairly long, rough route across Galway Bay. So not just any kind of hired boat will do. I think I'll have to go into Ros a' Mhil and ask around. Find a local to take us across, for payment under the table."

"And how will we pay them?" I asked. "We have nothing."

Louis held up a finger. "In that regard, my powers of persuasion *may* come in handy."

Remembering the fiasco with the letter from our father—how Louis had managed to hoodwink us with something he called a "confoundment spell"—I wanted to ask him what else his powers entailed. But Moira interrupted.

"Okay, then who of us should go into town?" she asked, standing up. Aidan shifted as if to join her, but another grimace crossed his face and he stayed put.

Good, I thought.

"I'll go alone," Louis said simply.

Despite her words back on the rustyback hill, her agreement that Louis should come with us, Moira was not so sure now. She stared at him, her lips in a thin line. Her long hours on horseback had clearly been spent in rumination. I wasn't sure what was going through her mind now, but she didn't look at me much. I was afraid my betrayal was foremost in her mind.

"I don't think that's such a great idea," she said softly. "I'll go with you."

"Yes, let's parade the wanted people through town, just in case there's someone there who's heard Medb's offer," Louis said, stalking away from the group to the edge of the woods.

"I'm not the wanted," Moira snapped. "Ríona is."

Louis whirled around. "But you *are* the one marked by the Blood Omen."

This silenced Moira, and my own heart skipped a beat. Silence descended on the little corner of forest that held us in its quiet fingers, waiting for us to make a move.

At long last, Louis walked back toward the group and stood opposite Moira. "You three are out of the question, and Aidan is injured," he said, his annoyance carefully controlled. "I will go, and I will do my best to find safe passage."

I knew what Moira's unspoken worry was. It was the same as my worry about Aidan: Could we trust them? Louis had fought for us back at the castle, but it was difficult to forget what we'd learned since then. Our last attacker, as he lay dying on the rustyback hill, had revealed Louis's real identity to us. He'd revealed that Louis had somehow been involved in Medb's plan to capture Ríona—who she believed to be this Morrigu—to regain some sort of power in Ireland. But then Louis had gone and defended our lives against those men. He said he no longer served this evil Queen Medb. But what if the long trek had served to change his mind about a few things? What if Louis went off to town and summoned one of Medb's henchmen? We would be tucked away here like sitting ducks with no idea that harm was on its way.

"If you didn't trust me," Louis said evenly, "why did you bring me along?"

Moira shook her head the tiniest bit and glanced at Conry. "Keep your friends close . . ."

A tiny smile quirked up the corner of Louis's mouth. "And your enemies closer? If that's proper protocol, I'm afraid we're headed in the wrong direction."

Ríona looked at me, her eyes wide, and then at Moira. "You know where Medb is?" I demanded.

"Does she have our father?" Moira shouted. "Is that how she found us? She tortured him?"

Louis shook his head. "I know where the seat of Medb's power is, but that's it." He raised his eyebrows—and his forearm. The triskele glared back at us. "And we need to get to the Aran Islands so we can figure out a way around this damned thing without being attacked from every direction."

"EVERYTHING'S going to be okay," Aidan said for the thousandth time since Louis had left for Ros a' Mhil. His hand was on Moira's back as she glared at Conry and fidgeted, rocking back and forth, leaves crunching beneath her. Conry hadn't budged from his spot at the edge of the forest, where Louis had ordered him to stay.

"Define *okay*," Moira grumbled. "Because I don't think it means what you think it does."

Ríona and I shared a weak smile. Moira's long-suffering attitude was like a comforting old blanket. To be fair, we were currently wandering the countryside with no home to return to, our very lives in the hands of a relative stranger with one too many secrets. *Okay* wasn't the word I would use for it either. Even without all the lies and secrets we'd recently uncovered, our situation would have made us uneasy. We didn't travel much, and isolated here in an unknown rural area, where very few locals looked like me or Ríona, it put us all on edge.

"Okay, okay!" someone shouted from the treetops. The squawk morphed into the unintelligible rantings of a crow, and I jumped to my feet. Finbar came swooping through the canopy of green.

"Jaysus, there you are!" I exclaimed. Finbar landed clumsily on my shoulder, and when he caught his footing I saw why—a big, shiny object was clutched in his beak, partly obscuring his sight.

"What is that, you filthy little thief?" I demanded, unfurling my hand. Finbar obediently dropped his booty into my palm. It was a small gold watch with a chipped face.

"Arah, and here we thought you were off protecting us, *oponu*," Moira said, rolling her eyes.

"He's not a fool!" I snapped.

"No such luck," Moira said to Finbar, ignoring me. "You were off hunting for trash."

Before I could give a smart reply, Faolan leapt to his feet, the fur on his back raised, and Ríona straightened, looking desperately around. It was rare that someone was able to sneak up on Ríona. My stomach flipped.

Conry stood just a moment before Louis ducked under the branches on the edge of the woods, shooting us a bright smile as he strolled our way.

Breathing a sigh of relief, I exchanged a glance with Ríona, who visibly relaxed. Finbar gave a relieved squawk. He'd surely felt my anxiety. I slipped the broken watch into my pocket and held a finger out for him to climb atop.

"Thank God." Moira sighed.

"It's not him you should be thanking," Louis said, all his cocky bravado back for the first time since he'd come scrambling through our kitchen window back at the castle just hours ago. "I managed to learn the name of a man who makes the journey to the islands often to see family and is garrulous enough to want the company of friendly American tourists." He winked at us. "That's us. You should hear my accent. It was superb acting, truly."

Aidan laughed. "I'd like to hear that."

"In due time," Louis said. "If we wait much longer, breakfast will be cold." He held up two plastic bags bursting with food.

"He's a god!" Ríona signed. It was lucky Louis couldn't understand ISL, I thought. The last thing he needed was more confidence. His ego was bursting at the seams already.

The bags were stuffed full of snacks from the shop—breakfast rolls, crackers, a handful of granola bars, some apples, and a few bruised bananas. I took a whole breakfast roll, the smell of eggs and sausage setting my stomach to rumbling. Settling back down on the moss-covered roots of a gnarled oak tree, I stuffed my mouth and tore a tiny piece of egg off for Finbar. He took it in his beak and hopped away to protect his treat while the others made their selections.

It was our first meal since we'd fled the rustyback.

"This is feckin' divine, Louis, truly," I said, hoping to lighten the mood, "but I would give many curios for this to be a roasted plantain instead."

"Or chin chin," Ríona signed, frowning at the bag of crisps she'd selected. *"Can you imagine a bit of chin chin right now?"*

Moira made a strangled sound in her throat and looked dreamily at the branches above us. "God, I can't take this! There'll be roasted plantains in my sleep tonight!"

Ríona giggled and gave a soft sigh. She and Moira had taken care of most of the cooking at home—I could never be bothered. Their favorite dishes to make were the ones that reminded us most of Mam. There'd been quite enough roasts and veg in our diet growing up, just like for most kids in Ireland, but Mam would hide away in the kitchen making her favorite Nigerian dishes when she was feeling especially homesick for her family and the little street in Dublin where she'd grown up among Nigerian immigrants.

My mind suddenly went to Ballyconneely, the small town nearest our castle, and all the people we saw at the market. Would any of them even notice we were gone?

"Do you think Farmer Sheehan will miss us?" Ríona signed, as if reading my mind. She'd always had a soft spot for the Sheehans. It was Mrs. Sheehan who had taught us all ISL—Irish Sign Language.

I sighed and closed my eyes, the castle rising up from the ground in my head. Emotion clogged my throat, and I cleared it. "Not as much as I'm going to miss that money-growing plant, j'know?"

"Are you sure you won't miss Brian Brennan more?"

Annoyance pricked at me, but Moira grinned. She wasn't trying to start a fight. It was just a glimpse of the old, playful Moira shining through. "Not as much as you'll miss those antlers," I said, grinning. One of Moira's favorite curios had been the antlers that gave its wearer a feeling of power. "Right when we could use a bit of control, like."

"Or a sense of it anyway," Moira agreed, nodding.

"I'm going to miss my room," Ríona signed, and she buried her fingers in Faolan's fur.

"I'm going to miss my room too," Moira said, staring at her lap.

"Me too," I said. Especially my giant bed and Finny's little nest. I clutched the watch he'd brought me tightly in my hand and thought of all the things that had burned with Bunrowan. The silence stretched on.

Finally, Moira brushed her hands off, a sure sign that she was done reminiscing. "Well, I guess we didn't know much of anything about our home, did we?"

"We still don't," I said. "What crown has Medb promised to the person who can bring Ríona to her? And why? How did we end up in the middle of this? We don't know anything."

Moira's response died on her lips as she and I noticed Ríona at the same time.

Ríona had straightened, her head turned toward the shadows behind us, just as Faolan climbed to his feet, the hair along his back standing once more.

an dia caillte
THE FALLEN GOD

ríona

I felt it in the trees. An energy. One that hadn't been there a moment before. Climbing to my knees, I froze. It was a few energies. A few disparate beings that were still and quiet. A steady beat of anticipation accompanied them. But they were hidden from view.

Hands shaking, I stood, and my sisters followed suit. They reacted immediately. We were woven together by years of history. Meanwhile, Louis and Aidan both looked around helplessly, fumbling with the remnants of their breakfast, slow and confused. It wasn't until Faolan unleashed a low growl into the shadows that Louis jumped to his feet and Aidan grabbed at a tree, trying to pull himself upright on his injured leg. Finbar squawked from Bríd's shoulder, and Conry ran to Louis, his throat rumbling in warning.

But it was too late.

The figures melting away from the shadows had us surrounded

before I could sign a warning to anyone. Not that a warning would have done much good. We were outnumbered and woefully underprepared for combat. The men and women who surrounded us now carried weapons, medieval weapons—swords, spears, and bows. A glittering, threatening aura encompassed them, one great big energy bent on violence. It was suffocating.

"What in God's name?" Moira breathed, backing toward Bó. The mare stood stiffly by a tree, her eyes darting around at the newcomers. Bríd and I both sidled toward her, eager to be near each other, and Aidan stumbled to be close to Moira. Only Louis stood apart, in front of us, glowering around at the ring of attackers. He put his hand out and stared at his palm, as if willing something to appear there. For a moment, the image of the great sword he'd had back at the castle flickered in his hand. But it was gone in the blink of an eye.

The attackers laughed, highly entertained by this display. There were six of them, and each looked a bit worse for wear. Like they hadn't seen a decent meal or a shower for quite some time.

One of the men stepped forward and grinned, showing a perfect set of tobacco-stained teeth. An aura of swirling red followed him, sparks flying off his shoulders. "We knew the minute we heard you jabberin' away in town that we'd found the runaway god hisself. Didn't we, Paddy?"

The squat man beside him let out a bellow, scratching his long, dirty beard. "'e fancies himself an actor, don't he? Like 'e don't stink of the *aos sí*." He stepped forward and poked at Louis with the end of his spear.

Conry snarled at the short man, who jumped backward but let out a shaky chuckle as the others laughed at him. "The old gods, almighty! They sure do think a lot of 'emselves, don't they?"

Louis's eyes flashed. "Who are you, and what do you want?"

The man with the red aura chuckled, the sparks growing larger. "If you have to ask that question, laddie, you lot are much too far behind for us to catch ye up now. You'll just have to come with us and see."

"We're not going anywhere with you," Moira said.

The man chuckled again. "The old gods always did like to make friendly with the more powerful, didn't they?" His friends found that uproariously funny for some reason. "Do share, lad." He poked at Louis again. "What'd you tell them to make them think you can help? A runaway god like yourself with no power to speak of . . . Why do they even keep you around?"

"Louis," Bríd said quietly, her energy pulsing quickly like an external, racing heartbeat galloping alongside my own. "What the feck is he talking about?"

Louis glared at the man, ignoring Bríd. As usual, I couldn't read anything on him. "I may be a fallen god, but I'm no runaway."

"No? Then what do you call this? Scurrying through the brush with the most wanted girl in Ireland, her sisters, and a . . . ?" He cocked his head at Aidan, his eyes narrowing. "An animal."

My heart lurched. Who was this man who knew what Aidan was just by looking at him? It was difficult to discern any individual's energy in the mass that was roiling around me now, a mix of emotions buffeting me and swirling together, but the particular danger coming off this man was as clear as day. It was a carefree recklessness searching for trouble at the cost of anything. A man who had nothing to lose.

"I call this defending myself," Louis cried. "Medb tried to have me killed."

"Arah, what's a few failed assassination attempts between friends?" The man shrugged, his brown-toothed smile making another appearance. But it slipped off his face just as quickly, and he twirled his spear around one hand. The others around him were shifting, stepping forward, growing restless.

Panicking, I looked desperately around me for some sort of weapon, anything to defend my sisters and our friends with. Bó stamped her hooves uneasily, and Finbar's inky black head turned this way and that, his beady eye surveying the scene. How could we get out of this?

The memory of a buzzing in my chest, just below my sternum, rose in me like a ghost. I hadn't even been trying back at the castle when I'd summoned the swarm of bees. If that was truly what had happened. My desperation and fear had simply coalesced into a power I didn't understand. Well, we were truly desperate now.

I closed my eyes, focusing on the feeling of my racing heart and the swirling energies that buffeted my senses like a storm and made my skin prickle with electricity.

Bees. Birds. Anything. Come on!

Nothing. That was what came to our rescue. Absolutely nothing. And it was absurd that I'd even considered the possibility. Who did I think I was? This Morrigu that everyone kept talking about? How had I let myself get swept up in this prophecy, these strangers' convictions that I was something more than an ordinary girl? This was all some giant misunderstanding. They were after the wrong girl. My sisters and

I didn't belong anywhere except alone in a tumbledown old castle beside the sea.

And even that was gone now. We had no unknown power. Only an unknown future.

"I won't let you take them," Louis said, stepping in front of me. Faolan stepped up beside him, my pair of knights in shining armor. "They are none of your concern. Leave Medb to do her own dirty work for once. You needn't risk your own necks for something she seeks."

The man with the spear took one step forward and cocked his head at me, a move so reminiscent of Finbar it sent a shiver down my spine. "That 'er then?" He looked me up and down. "A little younger than I was expecting, to be honest. But I guess it won't be mattering none in the end. Which is near, laddie, I assure you that."

His spear came forward fast, and Faolan reared to take the blow. *No!* The word exploded in my head, every nerve ending in my body vibrating with the sharp pain of uselessness.

And that was when it happened.

A storm of beating wings and shiny black eyes descended upon us, obscuring my vision. The confused cries of our attackers were followed by cursing and wailing as they beat at the air, which was now thick with wings.

Thick with tiny black creatures that chittered and squeaked.

Bats.

We had to act now, but I couldn't move. I could only stand there in shock. I'd done this. I knew it. I could feel it. I could feel *them.* The bats, their tiny hearts beating as fast as their wings, my anger, my fear, my desperation flying around my head, manifest in their tiny bodies.

"Ríona!" Moira's scream broke through my daze, and I saw her already upon Bó's back. Just feet away, Bríd yelled for Finbar, her head thrown back toward the sky, and Louis, with a murderous gleam in his eye, advanced on the man with the spear.

Moira's hand was outstretched toward Aidan, but his hand was in mine. In one swift movement, punctuated with only a small limp, he tugged me toward Bó and pushed me onto her back. I climbed up behind Moira and before I could reach down to see if Bó could handle a third rider, Aidan gave Bó a firm pat on the hindquarters and the True Mare sprang into action.

"Wait!" Moira yelled, but Bó ignored her. We dashed past Louis, who was locked in a stumbling dance with the man with the spear, both latched on to the weapon in a battle of wills. Bó ran right through the unbroken circle of attackers, who still swatted at the bats cutting through the air, and we took down a few disoriented men.

"Aidan!" Moira screamed. "Bríd!" But Bó didn't slow. She would get Moira to safety at all costs.

Faolan, I said, without turning around. *Come to me. To safety.*

A deep answering howl went up, and a calmness settled over me. The attackers' auras dissipated from my consciousness as Bó put distance between us. When we broke free of the canopy of trees, Bó cantered for a moment and then ducked back into a nearby copse. Here, she stopped, stamped her hooves uneasily, and went still.

"We shouldn't have left them," Moira whispered, her voice breaking. "But I was ... God, Rí, I was scared. With Bríd's premonition, I hardly thought twice about fleeing."

She wasn't looking at me, so I gently touched her shoulder. There was danger everywhere now, and she couldn't bear the responsibility of keeping us safe any longer. All of us had to play a part.

A rustle in the trees made us both start. Moira slipped off Bó and grabbed a nearby branch, ready to fight. I jumped to the ground beside her, closed my eyes, and tried to discern the energy of the creature coming toward us. It was a split, dual aura—

Aidan stumbled into sight and collapsed against a tree when he saw us. Faolan was at his heels, Louis and Conry just steps behind. Aidan doubled over to clutch his shin, pain etched in his face.

"They're gone," Louis said, his chest heaving as he stopped beside Aidan and put a hand on his shoulder. "We thought they would overpower us, and we started to run, but they didn't come after us."

"What?" Moira demanded. "They didn't come after you? Why?"

"Bríd?" I signed furiously at Moira. *"Where's Bríd?"*

trip
FAILURE

moira

Every one of us froze. Listening. Straining to hear anything. Anything that would tell us Bríd was nearby, and alive. But all was utterly silent.

Without another thought, I hurtled myself onto Bó's back and galloped in the direction from which we'd come.

"Moira, wait!" Both Louis and Aidan called after me, but I didn't slow. Neither did Bó.

In just moments, Bó pulled up short at the area surrounded by flattened underbrush and the litter of our breakfast. The space was empty.

"Bríd!" I screamed. "Finbar! *Bríd!*"

Tears streaming down my face, I slid off Bó's back. *"Bríd!"*

Faolan reached me, his nose to the ground, but he made it only halfway across the clearing before he turned back around and made several confused swirls. Too many people had been here.

Ríona arrived next, her chest heaving, her eyes filled with fear. She grabbed my arm and shook her head. *"I can't feel her,"* she signed.

Louis and Conry appeared, and then Aidan, limping and pale, but they were all too late. We were all too late. The tears poured down my face. I had failed in the only thing I'd ever felt destined to do.

I had failed to protect one of my sisters.

The others looked silently around the wood, and Faolan gave a whimper. He dug something out of the earth and turned to Ríona, who held out her hand to take the object from his mouth. She held it up— the small gold watch Finbar had gifted Bríd this morning. The others slowly realized what no one would say out loud.

Bríd had been taken.

curtha i sáinn

A TRAP

a i d a n

Moira was running toward Bó again.

"Wait, Moira, stop!" I yelled as loudly as I could. Which wasn't very loud at all. My lungs felt weak and empty. Pain lanced up my leg, and I knew I wouldn't be standing much longer.

"We have to go after them!" Moira screamed. She was nearly hysterical, and I didn't blame her. I knew the guilt she would be feeling for getting on Bó and riding off in the middle of a fight. But the risk had been too great. As Louis had said, it was Moira whose future had been marked by the Blood Omen. I didn't know what it meant, but if Louis was to be trusted—and I was starting to suspect he was, to a degree greater than any of us understood—Moira was in just as much danger as her sisters.

"Moira—" My leg gave out, and I fell against the nearest tree as Moira clambered onto Bó's back. Would the True Mare let her girl ride

into danger? She was supposed to protect her rider. My heart hammered in my chest, but I didn't have to wait to see. Because Louis stepped in front of Bó and placed a hand on her muzzle.

"You riding off after them, that's exactly what they want," Louis said. "It's a trap."

"Yes," I said, warming to the theory. "It's Ríona who Medb really wants." I glanced at Ríona, who looked distraught and too preoccupied to weigh in or even try to stop Moira.

"Exactly," Louis said, patting Bó as Moira glared down at him. "Those scoundrels, they know that you and Ríona won't let your sister be taken. They know that you'll come after her. They've obviously fallen back to set a trap to lure you two in. If I know Medb, she'll lay the trap herself. So, you, riding off without a plan? That is exactly what they want."

I remembered what Louis had done back at the castle—the "confoundment spell," he'd called it. To trick the girls into believing his handwriting was actually their father's. Was that really possible? And if so, was he doing something similar to Moira now?

Moira snorted. "So we're just supposed to let them take her?"

Well, if he was trying to persuade her with some sort of magic, it definitely wasn't working this time.

"No," Louis said evenly. "You will go after her. But not until we're ready."

Moira heaved two deep breaths, her nostrils flared. "And if they hurt her in the meantime?"

Images floated through my mind as I tried to imagine where they would take Bríd. What they would do to her.

"You have evaded capture twice now," Louis said, his eyes steady on Moira. "And Queen Medb will not take that lightly. Now that her best men have failed, and her second-best men have failed, her best bargaining chip is Bríd. She will not be harmed."

I waited, my leg throbbing, for some sign of what Moira would do next. I knew if she decided to go after her sister, there would be no stopping her. But she had to see the foolishness of it.

Moira looked at Ríona. At this point, Ríona would be the only one who could stop her sister from riding into certain danger.

Ríona signed something that made Moira sigh. She turned to Louis. "So, what do you propose we do?" she asked him. Bó stomped nervously.

"We continue," Louis said simply. "We go to Aidan's father, and we seek assistance in coming up with a plan. A plan to rescue your father . . . and your sister."

Moira looked at Ríona once again. The sisters shared another silent exchange, with Ríona's fingers flying in ISL. I tried to read the emotions on each sister's face, but there was little I could discern apart from anguish. Had they ever been parted from each other before?

Finally, Moira's gaze turned on me and back to Louis. "We'll go to Inis Mór and try to come up with a plan to rescue Bríd. But we won't wait forever. When we decide it's time to go, whether we have a plan or not, we go." She nodded at Louis. "And you will lead us there."

Louis paused only a moment before nodding his agreement. I didn't know how he could make that promise with the triskele oath binding him to secrecy. But that was a concern that could wait.

"Thank you," Louis said, taking a step away from Bó. "This is the best course of action for rescuing your family; I know it. And just maybe the best way to defeat Queen Medb."

Biting her lip, Ríona signed something to Moira, who nodded agreement and cast a scathing look at Louis.

Louis glanced between them, his eyes landing on Moira in search of a translation, his eyebrows raised.

Moira tipped her chin up, the thin line of her lips becoming even thinner. "Ríona noticed you call her *queen*."

The glimmer always present in Louis's eyes dulled, and he went still, unnaturally still, like a wax statue of himself. Finally, he cleared his throat and turned. "Old habits die hard."

an ardchathair
THE CAPITAL

bríd

The first thing I felt was something solid slamming into my left side. Something freezing cold—and covered in gravel. My head felt like it had been blown full of wind and then deflated. I gasped for breath, and the air seared my throat. The noise of a crowd was loud and close, but I could see nothing. Nothing but blackness.

And then I remembered.

I was blindfolded, arms bound, in the hands of our enemy. At least, one group of them. Sent by our biggest enemy of all. The evil Medb.

My arms shaking, I reached my bound hands out and felt sharp, dry grass, dirt and rocks between my fingers. I tried to push up to my knees, but the gravel ate into my palms, and I collapsed back to my stomach, my tied hands useless beneath me. I felt vaguely nauseated. What had they given me to knock me out?

All around me was the buzz and chatter of people. A lot of people.

Hundreds, if I wasn't mistaken. Was I in the middle of a city center? Ballyconneely wasn't big enough to create this sort of hum. In fact, the only place big enough was Galway city itself. Which wasn't all that far from Bunrowan Castle, but I would still have a hard time finding my way home.

Not that we had a home for me to return to. How would I ever find my sisters again?

The barking of dogs broke through my thoughts and then the exasperated groan of a cow. It was followed by a chorus of its fellows answering its cry.

Cattle? Not Galway, then.

The smell of smoke and the stench of livestock stood out from the concoction of smells around me. As the call of dogs and livestock mixed with human voices, I strained to try to pick out newly familiar voices in all the noise. Were my kidnappers nearby?

The cloth was ripped from my eyes, and sunlight seared my retinas.

They squeezed shut instinctively, and somebody close laughed. Squinting into the brightness, I looked up. There was nothing in front of me but a series of large earthen mounds and the sprawling green hills of the Irish countryside beyond. My kidnappers pulled me to my feet as I looked wildly around.

No one was behind me except my small band of kidnappers, who chuckled at my confusion. I heard people, animals, the clang of metal. But the hills were empty.

Except for myself and these eejits, there was no one.

The noises of a bustling town, of country life, were blooming out of thin air.

"Welcome to Cruachan, little Morrigan," the large one said, sneering down at me.

And then, with one good shove, he pushed me across a ditch in the earth, and the trench drew my feet out from under me. I toppled to my hands and knees once again. Blowing a strand of dark hair out of my face, I pushed up with my bound wrists and struggled back to my knees. And froze.

Unfurled before me was a bustling town.

I stared.

My sisters and I had seen and experienced and heard too many strange things to count. But I was very sure that there was a town laid before me now that had not been there moments before.

This was no castle curio. No premonition or flighty dream. This was a magic I didn't understand.

The trench I knelt in now was a dirt pathway that encircled a great deal of the town, from what I could see. The town was crowded with wagons, horses pulling carts and chariots, people trudging along on foot, and children running. They wore rustic tunics, heavy furs, and primitive shoes.

The earthen mounds I'd first taken for another desolate patch of Irish countryside sported great wooden and stone structures atop them. People and animals of all kinds climbed up and down the hills and even crouched around open fires that dotted the landscape. Smaller wooden roundhouses sat in clusters in the shadows of the great hulking mounds, and streams of smoke escaped the cracks of roofs made of straw and mud.

"Where the feck are we?" I whispered to the wind.

"Capital of Connacht," my kidnapper said, nudging me. "On yer feet now."

Still openmouthed, I managed to find my feet without losing balance again. A man dragging a donkey along by the bridle looked sideways at me, but nobody else paid us much mind.

"*Where* are we?" I asked again. After all, there was no capital of Connacht. And I was a lifelong resident of the westernmost province in Ireland. I would know. There were people of all kinds around me—white, Black, different shades of brown. I even spotted a girl who didn't look very unlike me.

"I told ya. Cruachan, the capital of Connacht," the man said, spitting in the dirt and nudging me forward between two horse-drawn carts. "And we've got places to be, so mind your step."

The man pushed me through the crowd, around the nearest mound, and across a grassy area where people had wares laid out for selling. Almost like our own market back home. Except these people were selling spears and bows and animal skins, and spices and herbs I didn't recognize. The people themselves were more diverse than any crowd I'd seen in Ballyconneely. There was a family with dark-brown skin selling bright bolts of cloth, and a bent old man with sickly white skin attempted to haggle over a rooster with a girl with olive skin and long, dark-brown hair. The man was angrily brandishing a crutch at her, but she merely huffed and walked away. My attention was so thoroughly stolen that I barely registered the world toppling over as my kidnapper shoved me forward.

I stumbled over a wooden plank set unevenly into the stony earth. My gaze tipped up the stairs and landed on a hulking stone structure atop what appeared to be one of the very largest mounds in the city. To my right, a glistening pond reflected the bright sun, and a bevy of guards talked and spit in the dirt to my left.

"*When* are we?" I whispered to myself.

"C'mon, there now," my kidnapper grumbled, passing me on his way up the stairs. "You wouldn't be the first prisoner to perish on the climb up this mighty mound. Ráth Cruachan, it's known as. But we can't let you go dying today, fortunately for you."

Another shove from behind told me my band of kidnappers was still intact. It had lost a few members, but a handful of men still brought up the rear with ugly sneers and the closest raised a hand in warning. Turning back to the steep stairs in front of me, I began to climb.

The sun beat down, and I wondered desperately if there was a way to keep from entering the building ahead. I didn't know where I was, or who these people were, but I had the feeling that if I disappeared through the carved wooden doors at the top of the stairs, I would be farther away from my sisters than I had ever been in my life.

Every time I stumbled, I earned another push from behind, and that brought me to the summit faster than I'd have liked. The two tall pine doors were thrown open to the Irish sun, and I could make out just the faint outline of wild beasts carved into the panels. A wolf howled in one corner, next to two creatures that could only be described as monsters. Before I could study the carving any closer, another shove sent me over the threshold.

I turned desperately back the way we'd come and was rewarded with a glimpse of shiny black wings against a bright blue sky.

Finbar, I thought furiously, hoping to will him away. *Go. Leave. Find Ríona and Moira.*

He was the last thing I saw before the doors slammed shut with a thud that shook my bones.

Steeling myself with a deep breath, I turned to look down a long hall with an arching timber ceiling. Scores of people in primitive clothing milled about, casting interested glances my way. And at the very end of the hall, atop a throne carved from wood the color of fire, sat a scowling woman with a black crown atop her head.

Don't linger here, Finbar, I thought. *It isn't safe.*

níos mó ceisteanna ná freagraí

MORE QUESTIONS THAN ANSWERS

moira

"How did we come to be here?" I breathed.

Louis's gaze was heavy on my face. "Your obstinacy."

That was fair enough. The soft snap of Bó ripping grass out of the earth brought me gently back to reality. This was how things were, and I would have to deal with it. Ríona was on a ferry making her way across this tiny corner of the North Atlantic with Aidan. I was staying on the mainland with Bó, Faolan, an ill-behaved dog, and a mysterious boy I couldn't trust as far as I could throw him.

He caught me looking his way. "Your obstinacy is largely to blame. But a horde of well-timed bats contributed as well."

I didn't return his smile.

"Moira, this is the best plan. I promise," he said solemnly.

"I'm not sure what your promise is worth at the moment," I said quietly as I turned away. But not before I saw him brush his fingers over the tattoo on his forearm.

In the end, it really had been my obstinance that had brought us to our current situation. We couldn't all go to Inis Mór—Bó would need to stay behind, and Faolan would be no help in escaping the locals' notice. When it had been proposed that I, the one with the mark of the Blood Omen, stay with the animals, I'd flatly refused. There was no way Ríona would be going to a remote island with only an injured Aidan to protect her from the relative stranger Louis, should she need protecting. I was, of course, surprised when Louis had agreed with me. He'd explained that he would support any arrangement as long as Ríona went—she would be safest if she was moving away from Medb's seat of power.

"And where is that?" I had asked.

He, of course, couldn't say. He'd only lifted his arm with that blasted tattoo.

My whole body ached from our journey, and I slipped to the ground, leaning my back against a bowing tree. "Well, I wasn't even asking how we ended up *here*," I said, gesturing at the woods around us. "I was asking how my sisters and I, three girls not biologically related, ended up living in a broken-down castle on the edge of the world?"

Louis sighed and claimed a seat in front of a tree across from mine. "That I couldn't tell you, even if I didn't have the triskele," he said quietly.

Any time I'd asked such things growing up, Dad had given some vague, flighty answer before changing the subject. "You sprouted right out of the ferns on the rustyback. Want some soup?" Or, "The faeries brought Ríona, the banshee dropped off Bríd, and you, my love, were a gift of the leprechauns." But Mam never played such games. Her answer was always the same: "You're mine, *Kehinde*, as sure as the sun will rise tomorrow."

I shook my head. It was past time we knew the truth. "This all started with Dad leaving. God, he never should have left us. He'll have questions enough to answer when we find him." My heart pounded in my ears as my mind said what my mouth wouldn't: *if we find him.*

The sounds of the forest filled the silence, along with Bó's gentle snacking on lush green blades of grass. Faolan sat nearby, his eyes fixed on an invisible spot on the horizon, no doubt where his girl was rushing away from him on a boat in the sea.

"I don't know the answers to all your questions," Louis said. "But I do know who you are. Who Medb thinks you three are."

The Morrigan, I thought helplessly. Having a title made this no easier to understand.

"And I believe her."

I frowned. *Of course you do.*

"And I promise I'll tell you what my part in this has been," Louis added, rubbing the mark on his arm. "As soon as I can."

an filleadh
THE RETURN

ríona

The water was choppy, and the ferry slipped and slid over waves taller than me. I was afraid I would be sick. How I wished Moira was with me! Moira always made me feel better.

Aidan was several rows in front of me, in deep conversation with an older gentleman. Both looked at home and content on the rocking and rolling boat, even as Aidan had his injured leg propped up on an empty seat. I couldn't tell what Aidan or the older man were feeling—there were too many people, too many auras crowding my mind, some as utterly miserable as I was—but the way Aidan incessantly tapped his fingers on his knee gave away his excitement.

Of course, it made sense. The waves had been his home for the past decade. And he was headed to see the father he hadn't seen in just as long. Aidan had told us his story, how he'd been sick and tried to escape death by resorting to his seal form. I didn't know whether my

stomach was more bothered by the rolling sea or the anticipation of meeting a selkie's family.

I bowed my head and breathed in deeply. How powerful I'd felt after we escaped the attackers in the woods. Those bats . . . it couldn't have been a coincidence. I'd felt them, deep in my soul. Their little hearts beating in concert with my anger. They had come at my call.

I just didn't know how I'd called them.

But I was feeling plenty weak now. We'd ended up on the public ferry after all, too scared to go looking for the man with the private boat for hire. It should have worried me, being so exposed. But there was some measure of comfort in being surrounded by tourists from every corner of the earth. There was a group of Black American tourists, their excitement tickling my fingers, seated up front. For a moment, I wished I were sitting with them. Not just sitting with them, but part of their group. Friends. Family, maybe. An older Black woman sat near the window, quietly watching the others with a serene smile. The sight of her sent a pang through my stomach—pure longing for my mother. A wave rocked the boat just then, dousing my gut in nausea once again. I gripped my seat.

A lump of grassy land came into view out the window to my right, and I breathed a sigh of relief. *Please be the right island,* I thought desperately, my stomach churning.

And it was.

People who were apparently familiar with this journey started moving toward the stairs to the top of the boat, leaving tourists and people like me staring out the window, queasy and reluctant to stand. My knees would buckle beneath me if I tried.

"Ready?" Aidan asked, appearing back in my row.

I nearly glared at him. I couldn't help it. His tone was too bright.

"You feeling all right?" he asked, shifting his weight off his bad leg.

Shaking my head, I stood and pushed past him. The sooner I was off this boat, the better.

Outside, bright sunlight shone on the people streaming down the long pier in front of us. I moved through the crowd, eager to be on solid ground, and then waited for Aidan to catch up.

"Okay, let's make a plan," he said, limping off in the direction of a small town at the base of the pier. "I've been here before, but I'm afraid I won't remember the way. My memories, from the time before, they're . . . cloudy sometimes."

My heart skipped a beat. How strange to think of his memories being divided into the before and after—before and after he'd taken to his seal form and lived in the ocean. The thought sent a shiver down my back. How had three ordinary girls like us found ourselves tangled up with people who lived and breathed fantasy? The kinds of fantasy I'd only ever read about in books.

I pulled a little notepad and pen from my pocket. Aidan had bought them off the man working the ferry ticket office; he'd been quite confused as to why Aidan was so desperate to buy a used notepad with the Galway flag on it and a pen with a chewed-up cap.

Where do we start? I scribbled hastily and shoved the notepad toward Aidan.

His excitement dimmed a little. Now that the crowd had dissipated, I could get a better sense for how he was feeling. His energy was mismatched, as usual, chaotic and strange on the inside even as his outward self was calm. Almost like there were two halves of him: the selkie and the human.

"Well, I remember a little shop here in the town. I think they could give us directions to Seamus's—my dad's—house. They knew him. It's ... it's actually where I met him when I came to ask for my sealskin."

Seeing his excitement falter, I felt guilty for being cold and pushy on the boat. Giving him an encouraging smile, I signed *OK* and gestured for him to lead the way.

He nodded resolutely and marched onward. But when he stopped outside the nearest shop, which really looked like no more than a shed, his face fell.

"It was here," he said. "It used to be a bike rental."

The shop definitely wasn't renting out bikes. It appeared to be selling ice cream. My stomach cried out for the agbalumo ice cream my mother used to make from scratch—her very favorite, courtesy of the African star apple. I could barely remember the taste, but just the thought of it filled me with warmth. That warmth was so intrinsically linked to my sisters that a coldness doused it immediately. We were so far apart now.

But the quicker we found Aidan's father, the quicker I could get back to them.

Aidan's chaotic aura was now twinned with a rapidly falling, deep blue haze. *"Let's try it anyway,"* I signed before remembering he couldn't understand ISL. Shrugging, I opened the door and gestured for Aidan to enter.

Inside the tiny shop, a middle-aged woman was helping two American tourists pick out flavors. When they finally paid and moved along, Aidan stepped up to the register, his back straight and his limp less pronounced. He was trying to be brave.

"Hello—" he started.

"Well, hello dears," the woman said brightly, her eyes flying between me and Aidan. There was the usual pause, the up-down path of her eyes on my body, the lingering on my hair. "Where are ye from?"

Her eyes waited on me for the answer. Forcing a tight smile, I turned to Aidan.

He saw the annoyance in my gaze and told the woman, "I'm from the US. She's from Connemara."

The woman's smile faltered. It's not like my sisters and I had traveled much, but you didn't have to travel far from home to get the stares and the questions. We were used to the disbelief. To being That Black Girl and That Asian Girl from Connemara. Once again, the pang of wishing I were in that big group of Black Americans overwhelmed me.

Aidan could see I was uncomfortable. He cleared his throat. "Do you happen to know the way to Seamus O'Leary's house?"

The woman bit her lip. "Oh, love. I'm so sorry to be the one who tells ye," she said regretfully. "Seamus O'Leary died some seven or eight years back."

Aidan's animal aura stumbled and slowed. Shock hung heavily around him. "It's okay," he said quietly. "We were kind of estranged."

The woman looked back and forth between the two of us. I almost reached a hand out to touch Aidan's arm, but panic distracted me. This was our plan. Our whole plan. How could we have hinged everything on the weak memories of a boy who hadn't been human in a decade? What would we do now?

"Though," the woman said, trying to sound bright, "if it's family you're looking for"—her uncertain gaze landed on me again, a small frown on her face—"it's some sort of relative of Seamus's that bought the house and is living there now. A nice couple, not from here." Aidan's mood didn't change, didn't brighten at the prospect, and the woman's energy wilted again.

Guilt flooded my gut. Aidan had just lost his father. Or at least he'd just learned that he'd lost his father years ago. I wasn't sure which would be more difficult to bear.

It didn't help that my own father could have passed some weeks ago now without my knowledge. I couldn't run the risk of losing my sister too. And Bríd was in danger. I had to follow the plan. For Bríd.

Could you tell us how to get there? I scribbled on the pad before holding it up for the woman to read.

Frowning more deeply at me, she said, "Um, yes," and outlined a vague route with troubling directions like, "Turn right at the yellow house, but the lemon-yellow one, not the golden-yellow one," and "Careful of the dog outside Joe's; he doesn't like strangers."

Aidan thanked her numbly before stumbling back outside.

On the street, the bright sunlight felt harsh. Before we moved on to Bríd's rescue, I needed to make sure Aidan was okay. I grabbed his arm, but he shook me off before I could write anything on the notepad.

"It's okay," he said. "It was a long time ago, and I didn't really know him. Let's go see who this relative is. I'm fine."

But the words didn't mean anything. Not when I could see and feel his anguish—in both sides of him, boy and selkie—as palpable as any I'd ever felt inside myself.

an bandia ardcheannais
THE SOVEREIGNTY GODDESS

bríd

My knees shook against the hardpacked earthen floor. I was flanked by just two of my kidnappers now. The rest had dissipated into the gathered crowd, eager to remain unseen by the fierce woman I faced.

She had pale white skin and hair the color of a starless night, her crown a thin band in the shining, depthless black of obsidian. She wore a bright red dress belted with golden rope and sat in a wide seat made of ebony, each arm supported by the face of a withering old man carved into the wood. The back of the throne rose halfway up the wall, strips of shiny burnt-orange wood rising like flames against a brown backing carved with swirls and knots. It was a chair fit for the chief of a powerful tribe or an ancient Celtic king. Not the evil woman who was hunting my family. A woman bent on our destruction.

Medb.

Everyone in the hall had fallen silent, and my heart pounded loudly

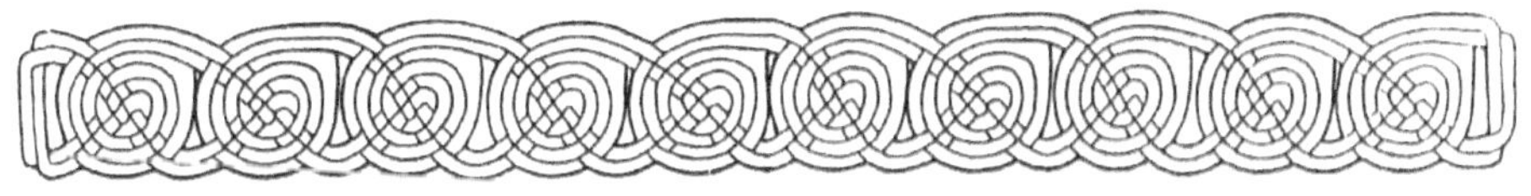

in my ears as Medb appraised me with icy blue eyes. She raised one thin, pale finger and gestured toward a girl standing in the shadows behind the throne. The girl was surrounded by several stern men who appeared at home in the shadows. They all seemed to have the same sharp chin, the same snide glint to their eyes.

The girl, who seemed no older than myself, stepped carefully through the throng of men and looked to the kidnappers on either side of me. She was as pale as her mistress but had blonde hair pulled back into a braid looped around the crown of her head. She wore a blue velvet dress that was leaps and bounds nicer than what the people outside had been wearing. Definitely not a servant. A long, thin animal skin was wrapped around her shoulders and fastened at the neck. Some kind of lady in waiting, perhaps? Ríona would have known, from all her feckin' fairy tales and storybooks.

"You are very welcome back to Cruachan," the girl said in Irish. Her eyes landed briefly on each man accompanying me, but her blue-eyed gaze was reserved and unfriendly, and it lingered, unexpectedly, on me. "You'll find the city fatigued and quite ruined with drink," she went on, her attention back on my kidnappers. "But that's only to be expected in the wake of Lúnasa."

Both men gave a polite chuckle. Our own Ballyconneely had a Lúnasa festival, too, but it was just a small party, certainly nothing to leave the whole town recovering.

"Please come forward," the girl said.

The men did so, each climbing one more step ahead of me. One of them fell to a knee, and the other awkwardly followed suit. "My queen, we return to you without the Morrigu, but not empty-handed." He hazarded a glance upward, but Medb wasn't looking at them. She was looking at me. The man threw a glance my way and then hastily continued. "As ye know by now, the sisters three have been provin' a bit more slippery than expected. With the help of Lú, they were able to flee after the siege on Bunrowan. In fact, it was by mere chance we found them at all, hiding out in a wood near the coast. They were attemptin' to reach Inis Mór, for reasons unclear."

He waited a beat, expecting Medb to say something. But she said nothing. She merely stared, unflinchingly, at me. I looked at the floor, the walls, the men behind the throne—anywhere but at the queen. I didn't dare meet those ice-blue eyes straight on while the wind in my veins twisted into tiny, painful tornados. I felt like I might lose control, my arms itching to do something—push myself off the floor, run, maybe strike something on the way. These people appeared to know Louis as "Lú." They knew exactly where to find my sisters. And there was nothing I could do about it.

"They escaped again when we attacked," the man went on uncertainly. "But we managed to get this one. The Morrigu's sister. Instead of going after the rest, we thought retrievin' you a little bait might be better."

Medb raised her hand, and the man fell silent. The hair on my arms rose in anticipation of hearing her voice. The voice that had commanded entire hordes to hunt me and my sisters.

At long last, she opened her mouth and said, "Look at me."

There was no question who she was addressing. Her voice was neither loud nor deep, a simple, middling tone that held firm and clear. Yet the command felt tangible—like a hand on my chin. Shaking with fear, I lifted my head and looked her in the eye.

"The spirit of Badb is very weak in you," she said.

And she waited. She looked into my eyes and waited for my struggling mind to work out what she'd said.

"I-I don't know who the feck you think I am," I said, my voice wobbling. Despite what the *bean nighe* had said—that the blood of the Morrigan ran through our veins—I couldn't believe it. I couldn't believe this Morrigan had anything to do with us. We would have known long before now. "And I don't know why you want my sister. But I do know we aren't whoever you think we are!"

The queen smiled, so serenely she could have been confused for a doting mother. Her lips curved upward, revealing two dimples in her thin cheeks. "I'm afraid it isn't who I think you are that is the issue. It's who I *know* you to be."

I gaped at her.

"Stand."

My knees knocking together, I slowly climbed to my feet. And I found that standing gave me back some control over my body. Standing, I felt like I could handle this. I could handle her.

"I've been searching for you a very long while," Medb said, tilting her head like a curious bird. Like Finbar when he spotted something shiny that he'd never seen before. "And it's probably long past time you learned what is truly at stake here."

I agreed it was long past time I learned everything. But this would only be everything according to Medb. How would I ever know if I could trust her version of the truth?

"You are in Cruachan," Medb said, lifting five long fingers to indicate the door behind me. "The seat of my power."

I swallowed. What power?

"For centuries, Cruachan was the capital of Connacht," Medb explained evenly. Her voice never wavered, never showed any emotion. "Ireland was ruled by four such sites, and Connacht was the most powerful of them all. My palace was here."

Between the plain stone walls, the murky light, and the hardpacked dirt floor, it certainly didn't look like a palace. Even more rudimentary than Bunrowan, a true castle for medieval chieftains.

Silence had fallen. Medb stared at me, not angry, not alarmed. But also not happy. Merely interested.

At long last, she asked, "Do you know who I am, *a leanbh*?"

If there were a better answer than honesty, I didn't know what it would be. So, pressing my lips together, I shook my head.

Her eyes never leaving mine, Medb held a hand out and waited. The girl with the golden hair hurried forward and took the queen's hand. The queen stood, and I saw that her feet were bare. She was not very tall, a thin woman, but a woman who knew her effect. She towered above us all.

"I am Queen Medb of Connacht," she said, her voice booming around the hall, "daughter of Eochaid Feidlech, High King of Ireland; warrior queen of Connacht; and sovereignty goddess of all Ireland."

Queen? King? Goddess? There were no rulers in Ireland. Around me, people had fallen to their knees. The strange men behind the throne and the golden-haired girl bowed their heads. My attackers bowed so far as to nearly touch the ground. I didn't know if it was out of respect or fear. Who were these people?

"No soul could rule Ireland without marrying me," Medb went on. "I held what they all longed for. The intoxication of true power. And occasionally destruction. I was the sovereignty goddess of my people." Medb's eyes had strayed to the ceiling, as though she were seeing something no one else could. A past no one else remembered. Except maybe the people on their knees before her. "Until I wasn't anymore." Her eyes fell back to earth—to me. "And I've been waiting centuries for you."

My heart hammered in my throat. It felt as though she were waiting for me to say something. Ask a question. Profess my fealty. Anything.

And I did have about a million questions. But only one came out of my mouth then: "Did you say *centuries*?"

That smile returned. Medb stepped backward and sat down on her throne, quirking her head. Her bare toes peeked out from under her dress. "The Morrigan, the battle goddess, a triplicate of extreme power. Unmatched, that's what they say. Hard to believe any of that as a helpless girl stands in front of me."

Helpless? I wasn't helpless. Not as long as I had breath.

"What does any of this have to do with me and my sisters?" I bellowed. "We never wanted any feckin' part of this! Why won't you leave us alone?"

"Badb, the Morrigu, and Macha. The sisters three. Each as fearsome as the next. But perhaps none so feared as the Morrigu."

"We aren't them!" I cried. "We'd never even heard of them before you started coming after us!"

Medb's stare was even, her silence calculating. And I could never have anticipated what she said next.

"Do you know what your father has done?"

My blood ran cold. Had Dad been here? Had he spoken to this woman, this "queen"?

"He made a deal, my dear child. He traded his pathetic soul and his daughters' safekeeping for a fortune. Your lives, your safety, for money."

No. *No.* What was she saying? That wasn't what we'd heard from the whispering pillow in Bunrowan: *And upon a day dark and dreary, at this kitchen table, did Brian Doyle sign away his soul for those of his ruthless daughters.*

My heart twisted. Was I really going to believe a pillow over the fearsome woman before me now? After all, Dad's disappearance had marked the end of our safety. Why had he left us?

I didn't trust Medb to give me those answers. But she was waiting for something. For a reaction from me. I wouldn't give her what she clearly wanted in this moment—emotion, passion, a broken heart. Instead, I simply asked, "What do you want from my sister?"

"It's quite simple, really," Medb said with a short sigh. "I may have once been the celebrated sovereignty goddess of Ireland, but the Morrigu has ties to the old reign too. It used to be said she could grant sovereignty or take it from kings with nothing more than a shriek."

That's what they thought Ríona could do? If only they knew their folly!

My kidnappers exchanged a quick look around me, and I realized they hadn't known the importance of what they were hunting. They didn't know this power that Medb believed belonged to Ríona. They simultaneously took a step back, their eyes wide at the talk of sovereignty and crowns.

Medb nodded at them. *"Déileáil leo,"* she said in Irish.

I spun around just as the scraping sound of metal sounded, followed by two strangled screams. Both kidnappers were slumped on the floor, two men behind them, bloody swords in hand.

"Agus an cailín," Medb said, nodding at me.

The two killers sheathed their bloody swords, and each grabbed one of my arms. My breath caught in my chest. But Medb's face held neither malice nor joy.

"Is féidir libh imeacht," she said. *You may go.*

comhaireamh
A RECKONING

ríona

The house was a plain white bungalow with windows facing the sea. Across the cracked road was a low stone wall, beyond which a rocky field led down to the wild waves of the bay. The sight made me homesick for our castle and the rustyback hill. Shoving the pain away, I turned back toward Seamus O'Leary's house. A goat bleated from the front yard, and in the driveway sat a beat-up blue car, a small, orange cat lazing on the hood.

We made our way up the walk, and I stood there, waiting for Aidan to make the first move. When he didn't, I stepped forward and knocked. It was only a few moments before the door swung open, revealing a handsome man who looked to be in his thirties.

More importantly, he looked just like Aidan. He had the same round, brown eyes and messy hair. And the same wild aura within him. The intense warm glow of welcoming curiosity that surrounded the

man turned swiftly to a mess of confusion, and Aidan was already launching himself into the man's arms by the time bright shock and delight bounced off him, mixing with Aidan's own chaotic energy.

"Aido?" the man gasped, pushing Aidan away so he could look into his face. Tears dampened Aidan's cheeks as he nodded.

A woman with a short brown bob and freckles appeared, alarm enveloping her like solid armor. It melted away in seconds. "Aidan?" she asked.

"Cora," Aidan said cautiously, everything in him pausing, waiting to see how she would react.

She was silent for one never-ending moment and then stepped forward and crushed him in a hug. It was short, awkwardly brief, and when she stepped back, she looked from Aidan to the other man, clearly unsure how to handle this shock.

"You're . . . you're both older," Aidan said quietly, smiling shyly.

The man laughed loudly and slung an arm around Aidan's shoulder. "And you're not!"

"Ríona," Aidan said, pulling me forward. "Meet my brother, Rory. And his . . . Cora."

"Wife," Rory said sheepishly. "We got married after finishing up university in Dublin."

"Congrats," Aidan said, but his smile didn't reach his eyes.

How strange it had to be, to greet your brother after a decade, having aged only a handful of days. I couldn't imagine not seeing my sisters for nearly a decade. And then to be reunited when they'd gone and grown up without me? It was unimaginable.

"You're about five years too late for a wedding gift," Cora said with a laugh. "We're an old married couple now." She had an open, honest aura, and an American accent tinted with Irish vowels, similar to Aidan's and his brother's. And Rory—in him, I felt the same hybrid energy that Aidan had. Was he a selkie too?

"It's nice to meet you, Ríona," Cora went on. "Please, both of you, come sit." She ushered us into a small sitting room full of plush but worn chairs. A piano was in one corner, but it didn't look like it had been used much.

"How did you end up here?" Aidan asked, gesturing around at the cozy little house. He was smiling, but a heaviness covered him, an underlying sadness. Was it for the father they'd lost? Or the years he'd lost with his brother? Probably both.

Uneasiness twisted my heart. The uncertainty of not knowing when I'd see my sisters again was a physical pain in my chest. I wanted nothing more than to get straight to the point, why we were here. There was no telling what Bríd was going through right at this moment.

"After college, we left Dublin to live in Galway," Rory explained. "And that's where we were living when we were notified that we'd inherited Seamus's house here on the island. We used to come out to see him when we were living in Galway."

"He was . . . he was kind, Aidan," Cora said, and Rory nodded fiercely.

"We didn't know him well," Aidan explained to me. "Seamus, our real father. Nor our birth mother. We were raised in the US by a couple who were the only parents we knew, and we didn't know about the selkie thing until . . ."

"Until I came along one summer," Cora murmured. "And toppled everything." The heaviness of their collective memory held untold stories.

"And we're glad you did," Rory said, squeezing her shoulder. "Anyway, I guess the old man took a liking to me and Cora on our visits out here, but we still never expected him to leave us the house."

"Or the goat, for that matter," Cora said with a laugh.

"Well, we decided in the end it would be a good move." Rory shrugged, almost guiltily. "Good for the soul."

I slid the notepad out of my pocket, ready to interrupt and get down to business, when Cora added, "And we wanted to be closer to Róisín."

"Who?" Aidan asked.

Rory exchanged a quick glance with Cora, and she looked at her lap, an awkward guilt hanging on her. Rory, for his part, though uncomfortable, radiated only warmth. Love. "We have a sister, Aido," he said carefully. "Cora and I met her here on the island. Just after you left. It's a long story . . ."

I put the notepad down. For the second time since we'd gotten here, Aidan's chaotic, animalistic energy slowed, nearly stopped. This place was full of surprises. I wasn't sure Aidan could handle many more.

"You'll love her, Aidan," Cora said quickly. "She's away at college in Galway at the moment."

"Aidan," Rory said, "did you come straight here?"

"Kind of," Aidan said. "I found myself out in Connemara, near Clifden. That's where I met Ríona here and her sisters. I was injured, and they let me stay with them until I could recover."

"You're limping," Cora remarked.

"Does that mean you aren't . . . healed?" Rory asked.

Aidan had been sick. He'd told us that. It was part of the reason he'd taken to his seal form all those years ago. A last-ditch effort to cheat death.

Aidan threw a small glance my way and shrugged. "I'm not sure. I feel fine."

Cora and Rory looked at each other, and then Rory nodded. "Okay. Well, that's a good sign. I want you to know we, uh, we saw Mom and Dad. We went back to Oyster Beach with Seamus and told them everything—about where you'd gone, who we are, *what* we are."

I was right. His brother was a selkie too. But his aura wasn't quite as wild as Aidan's. Maybe it was a product of Aidan's years at sea. And what about Cora? How had she gotten tangled up in their story? Was it anything like how Aidan had gotten tangled up in ours?

"You mean they don't think I'm still out there traveling the world, or dead in a ditch?" Aidan asked, shaking his head. "Sometimes I can't believe how selfish I was to leave like that."

"No, Seamus helped us explain everything," Rory said. "And they understood, truly. We spent some time there. Seamus even saw Lia again. They talked. Before she went back to the sea for good." Rory shrugged. "But Cora and I, we always knew we'd come back to Ireland. To Inis Mór. We wanted to be as close to the water as possible. Just in case . . ."

Just in case Aidan came back. I didn't know their whole story, but I knew enough to understand that. Back at the castle, Aidan had told us he'd been gone more than nine years. That meant Aidan's brother had been sitting here on a tiny island, waiting for him, for nine years.

Aidan realized it too.

The guilt hung heavy and thick around his shoulders. It seeped into my bones. I didn't envy this realization of his, that he had controlled his brother's life so thoroughly, that decisions he'd made had shaped his brother's path.

But I had decisions to make that would affect my sisters' lives. And they couldn't wait any longer. I scribbled onto the notepad: *We need to hurry.*

As I handed it to Aidan, the constant symphony of the sea outside was broken by a pitiful wail from the depths of the house. Jumping up, Cora hurried out of the room and returned less than a minute later with a baby in her arms.

The look on Aidan's face, the way his whole being froze, his energy swirling to a halt once again, made me wish I were anywhere but here. This was an intrusion I couldn't stomach.

"Meet your niece," Rory said, scooping the baby from his wife's arms and placing her in Aidan's lap. His arms went around the tiny form, clumsy and unsure. "Lia."

Aidan gulped, and his eyes shone. "After our birth mother," Rory told me.

Never taking his eyes off the baby, Aidan asked, "Is she . . . ?"

I could guess what he wanted to know: *Is she a selkie?*

"We don't know yet," Rory said reaching out and taking Cora's hand. "We're a bit afraid to find out."

A thin ribbon of excitement slithered around the baby like a snake, intertwined with a soft gray fog of calm. It acted just like Aidan's aura.

And Rory's. I touched Aidan's arm, and when he looked at me, I nodded.

"You think she is?" he asked carefully.

Squeezing his arm, I nodded more forcefully.

Rory and Cora looked back and forth between us. I could tell they found my silence, probably my mere presence, strange. But I was used to people finding me and my sisters strange, especially me and Bríd. Cora opened her mouth to ask, "How—"

"They know things," Aidan said quickly. "Ríona and her sisters. They . . . they're special too."

Cora's hands went to her mouth as she smiled at me, excitement glittering off her.

"That's why we're here," Aidan said. "When I was at sea, well . . ." He took a deep breath and watched his niece wrap tiny fingers around his own. "It nearly defies description. Because I started to forget. Everything. Sometimes still, things from before are . . . muted. Like I'm not sure they really happened. And the time I was out there, it was living pure and simple, in the most primitive form. And my memory . . . well, it feels more like a dream than anything.

"Eventually, though, things began to change. I could feel it. It was like my human form, my reasoning, was intruding, forcing itself to be heard. A reckoning was happening, a reckoning of the land that rippled through the sea. It's so hard to explain, but it was like an invisible force was shaking the sea floor, except you could only feel it in your bones."

I hadn't heard Aidan say all of this aloud. I couldn't help but wonder . . . did this reckoning he'd felt in the sea, did it have anything to do with us? With me and my sisters, and the people hunting us?

Surely not.

"All the creatures knew something was happening," Aidan went on. "Fear reigned. Life was fleeing the waters around Ireland. Eventually, I did too. I climbed ashore, desperate to escape. But then I got to land, and that didn't feel safe either. And that's why we're here."

"To escape Ireland?" Rory asked, confused.

"No," Aidan said softly, glancing at me. "Somehow, I don't know . . ."

I had already scribbled down what I knew Aidan was thinking and lifted the notepad for them all to read:

I think we're supposed to save it.

iníonacha

DAUGHTERS

bríd

It was a jail cell. Plain and simple. A dark, damp box carved into the mud of the hill beneath Medb's palace. One wall was open to the road, barricaded with thick iron bars. Life went on outside, but this appeared to be a little-used road. The handful of people who walked by took no notice of me. The big striped box of moonlight that fell through the bars illuminated the stamped metal tray by the door that held an untouched piece of brown bread.

Tears streamed down my face as I stood in the cleanest corner I could find, just beside the bed of hay. This was the only position where I couldn't be seen from outside. Eyes closed, I perched on one leg, the other pulled up to rest against my thigh, and took deep breaths, trying to calm my churning insides. Desperately, I tried to remember if there was some sort of curio from home that I could recreate here. After all, Louis had said we were the ones creating the curios, not the castle. My

stomach growled ravenously. Opening one eye, I glared at the bread, alternately despising their pathetic act of charity and yearning to eat it. After all, I had to live to make them all regret this. To find my sisters and make everyone in this city pay.

A soft squawk from outside the bars made me jump.

I hadn't been expecting it, but I would know that squawk anywhere.

"Finbar!" I cried, rushing to the bars. He was down in the corner, and I fell to my knees, shoving my fingers through the bars to feel his silky-smooth feathers. "You feckin' bird! Why are you here? How did you find me? You have to leave, Finny!"

He was nestled in the grass on the other side of the bars and merely quirked his head at me. The sight was so like the Queen Medb, I shivered.

"Jaysus, you have to leave!" I cried, the tears falling faster now.

He squawked again and gently stabbed my palm with his beak. Then he bent his head and picked a small pink flower from the grass. He dropped it into my palm and nudged the lifelines there with the side of his beak.

"You feckin' eejit," I murmured through tears, curling my fingers around the flower. "What would I do without you?"

I didn't mean to, but it was so much warmer here where the light came in, and I was so tired. So very tired. And so I fell asleep with my fingers twined through the bars of my cell, Finny nestled against my skin.

I DIDN'T dream of Moira dying that night. I dreamed of our father. Of Bunrowan falling. Of Dad watching, wailing and screaming and crying for his daughters' safety as he saw what his leaving had wrought. I watched him cry and beat his fists against the ground, and I was angry with him. For walking away from us, again and again, until one time, he didn't come back. And, most importantly, for everything he'd never told us.

Our identities. This legend of the Morrigan. Were we really in some way related to this goddess of legend?

And had he actually traded his soul and our safety for a fortune? Because our safety had certainly evaporated when he'd left us.

Suddenly, the wailing of my dream father felt like the guilt of a man who knew he'd made the gravest of mistakes.

WHEN I finally awoke, my body fell to the ground with a dusty thump. I'd been levitating again. The pink flower was crushed in my palm. And Finbar was gone. I sat up and listened to the noises outside the cell. A variety of animals, and people speaking Irish and English and languages I didn't recognize, and children laughing, and the general cacophony of a bustling town. But the street outside my cell was empty.

Except for one person.

A girl. Walking toward me.

Her blue eyes shone bright in the sunlight. The queen's right-hand woman. She deftly opened the door to the cell, stepping inside with a tray on her hip.

She stood tall and proud, and my eyes fell to the veritable feast she'd brought. Not to mention the jug of liquid. My mouth cried out for water. "You haven't eaten," she said, looking at the untouched bread beside the door. There was surprise but little warmth in her voice.

"Wasn't hungry," I said lamely. My stomach growled in response, and I hoped she didn't hear.

She placed the new tray beside the other and said, "I am Findabair, the daughter of Medb, warrior queen of Connacht, sovereignty goddess of all Ireland, and daughter of Eochaid Feidlech, High King of Ireland. But you may call me 'Fenora,' as my father calls me and now most others too."

"You're her feckin' daughter?" I repeated stupidly. I couldn't imagine having the cold woman on the carved throne as a mother. Thoughts of my own mother flooded my mind. Her warm hands as she'd brushed my hair, rubbed dirt off my face, or tucked me into my big bed in the great hall on the sixth floor of our castle. *"Can you hear it?"* she'd say, just before standing up. *"The musicians are playing. Let them play you to sleep,* Taiwo. *"*

How I wish you were here now, Mam, I thought desperately.

"Is there anything else you need for your comfort?" the girl asked, interrupting my thoughts.

"Comfort?" I repeated sardonically. "Back home I slept in a cold, barren, stone fortress, like, but at least there I didn't have bars on my windows."

Fenora's mouth twitched. "Well, if you can think of anything else, I can come to you again later."

I stared at her. My eyes narrowed. "Why are you being so nice to me?"

Fenora paused with her hand on the door. "No one in their right mind would refuse Badb anything," she said. And then she left.

múintir ní chonaola
FAMILY OF THE CONNEELEYS

ríona

"Is this the best idea we've got?" Rory asked as we approached a tiny cottage overgrown with nettles.

Cora looked sternly at her husband, who was radiating unease. "Biddy Nolan is a kind, generous woman, and she's the best hope we have of finding someone on the island who knows about selkies already. Don't give credence to rumors."

"What rumors?" Aidan asked. He too was cloaked in nervous energy.

"That she's a *bean feasa*. A wisewoman who can see the future."

"That doesn't sound bad," Aidan said.

"Sure." Rory shrugged. "If you're not the type to be afraid of witches."

"Honestly, Rory!" Cora snapped. "She's not a witch. She's a misunderstood old woman who knows more about this island and this

country than anyone I've ever met. Only small-minded people are scared of what they don't understand."

Silently, I hoped this opinionated American woman was right. For the sake of my sisters and our future.

She wasted no time rapping on the door of the cottage, as if lingering too long would cause the brothers to lose their will.

The old woman who answered the door had clearly lived through every storm since the beginning of time. Her white hair was a messy nest, big enough to house Finbar, and her pale white skin was cracked like old concrete. A bright halo of curiosity surrounded her, almost too bright for me to look at, and wisps of deep purple lazily floated around her head. I couldn't get a clear feeling from them, just . . . *purple*.

Was this the aura of a witch?

"Hello, Biddy," Cora said brightly. "We need to talk to you about something serious. Can we come in?"

Biddy said nothing but smiled hugely, revealing three missing teeth. She was bent nearly double, and the simple brown dress she wore was ripped and torn and sewn back together in so many places, it looked to be covered in a giant white cobweb. She turned and shuffled back inside her house, which was apparently an invitation for us to follow.

The cottage was stuffed full of . . . *things*. I followed Aidan down the narrow path between the piles of random items. I assumed there was furniture beneath the mountains, but it remained hidden. Hidden by newspapers, books, rotting plants, torn clothing, dinnerware, crumpled paper, seashells, and other debris from the sea, all piled up, creating hedgerows on either side of us. Biddy led us calmly down this path to a tiny kitchen.

She gestured toward a sloping wooden table, covered in books and papers, and we all took seats around it.

She stood in an empty patch of floor near the cluttered stove and turned to us. "What can Biddy do for ye?" she asked. Her voice was like an ancient wooden door creaking open for the first time in a century.

Rory looked nervously to Cora, who rolled her eyes. "Biddy," she said, pasting a smile on her face, "this is Rory's brother, Aidan, and his friend Ríona. They need your help. But first there's something we need to tell you. Rory and Aidan, they're—"

"*Múintir Uí Chonaola*," Biddy said. "Family of the Conneeleys. I knew it surely the moment I set eyes on your *Ruairí*."

We all exchanged a confused look, except Cora, who waited patiently for Biddy to go on.

"Inis Mór is full of Conneeleys," Biddy said, nodding. "Descended, some say, from the seal folk of old. They could transform from human to seal form at will. Thanks to a sealskin with powers beyond understanding of man. But if ye are coming to old Biddy for help, I'd guess ye already knew that."

Rory and Aidan gaped at her. Cora smiled, vindicated. It was at her insistence that we had come to see this woman.

"But why have you come back?" Biddy was staring at Aidan, and his frantic internal aura stilled.

"How did you know?" he whispered.

"You reek of the sea, lad," she said, wrinkling her nose. "But why, after choosing the sea, would you spurn her?"

Gulping, Aidan started to explain. About the trouble he could feel brewing in the water and the earth. Biddy listened intently, her face betraying nothing. When he finished, Biddy turned to me.

"And you," she said. After her eyes ran the standard path over me from head to foot, her gaze drifted to the air around me, as though she could see an aura there. "You hold something strange within you. Who are you?"

I was used to loaded questions like this. *Where are you from? What are you?* But it didn't feel like she was asking me that.

I appraised the old woman again. At the debris climbing around her. Honesty, kindness, and wisdom shone from her like a golden summer sun. But more than that. The wisps of purple surrounded her like tiny phantoms, her own galaxy of little ghosts. There was something *strange* within her too. I thought of the bees and the bats, and of the power I'd felt in my veins when I'd realized *I* had done that. It was time to own it.

Retrieving my notepad, I scribbled away. Aidan's nervousness grew larger, more oppressive, as he read over my shoulder. Finally, I raised the notepad.

Biddy's watery eyes squinted as she read aloud, "'The Morrigu.'" Her eyes widened, and the purple wisps shivered.

Flipping the notepad around, I continued. Biddy read over my shoulder, "Someone powerful thinks I'm the Morrigu. But we don't know what that means." Biddy gasped. "Ye don't know the myth of the Morrigan?"

I shook my head, Aidan doing the same on the other side of the table.

Biddy sighed. "The Morrigan is a goddess of old Ireland. A

goddess of three, from the Otherworld, with the power to choose kings and fell armies at her will. Badb, the battle goddess; Macha, goddess of the land; and the Morrigu, the goddess of sovereignty."

And someone thinks we are them? I wondered, my heart racing.

"If you are the Morrigu, my child . . ."

I shook my head, and Biddy fell silent, as if following my command. With the bees and the bats, I'd almost believed it. I'd wanted to believe it. But now, hearing the words laid out so plainly, I cowered.

"They say Badb has the power to control whole armies," Biddy said softly, testing to see if I'd interrupt again. But I was too thirsty for answers. "And Macha, she has healing powers. And the Morrigu, of course, the Morrigu makes kings."

But this was the stuff of fairy tales. Not real life.

"Most say the gods of old have disappeared," Biddy said with a sad shrug. "But there are those who worship them still. Who is to know when a god is gone, truly?"

"And someone thinks Ríona and her sisters are those . . . those goddesses?" Rory asked.

Cora must have read the anguished confusion on my face. "Maybe we should go," she said urgently, touching my hand. But Aidan wasn't finished.

"Biddy," he said, "there's one more thing. . . . What do you know of a Queen Medb?"

Biddy looked confused for a moment, as if unsure why we would ask. "She's an old queen of Ireland. No one knows if she was a real historical queen, or merely a myth. There's a spot at the site of an ancient city, Cruachan. It's in County Roscommon. Some think the remaining Tuatha de Daanan, the gods of old, linger there still. And it's where Medb's throne was said to be located, millennia ago."

I reached across the table and several piles of books to grab Aidan's arm. That could be where they'd taken Bríd! Excitement rolled off Aidan in shivery waves.

"Ye know," Biddy added, tapping her chin as she looked at me, "that's also where they say the Morrigan comes from. A cave there, called Owneygat. They say it's where you—or rather, the goddess—first crawled out of the Otherworld."

Aidan squeezed my hand back.

"The Otherworld can still be accessed through Owneygat on Samhain. Or," Biddy said, turning to Aidan, "as you Americans call it—Halloween."

I grabbed the notepad again, but Aidan voiced everything I was thinking: "That has to be where Medb is," he hissed at me. "And where they've taken Bríd. Maybe it's where they have your dad too."

A leathery hand clamped down on Aidan's shoulder. "Lad," Biddy said, interrupting his excitement, "touch this."

She held out a small, dirty vial filled with an amber liquid.

Aidan seemed too shocked to argue. He lifted one finger to the glass and waited for Biddy to say something.

She gazed into the vial and then raised her eyes to meet Aidan's. Her golden glow softened, the purple wisps slowing, and sympathy emanated from her. "I may be denied a Christian burial for it, but that's the price I'll pay for helping to save a life. If your friend truly is the Morrigu, lad, you must find the Macha and ask for her healing powers. Your illness runs deeper than that gash on your leg."

Aidan looked away from her, and Rory closed his eyes. Biddy pocketed the vial.

Rory murmured, *"Go raibh maith agat.* Thank you, Biddy." Aidan stood to leave.

cruachan
CRUACHAN

bríd

I awoke with a start, my nose inches from the ceiling of my cell. With a gasp, I fell like a rock, hitting the hay with too much force to avoid pain.

"Feck," I mumbled, rolling onto my side. Luckily, the ceiling wasn't very high. Otherwise, I'd break my back with the way things were going.

I'd dreamed of Dad again. And his agony. Whether it was a vision of something to come, or a simple dream, I didn't know. But that didn't change that my anger at him for getting us into this mess coiled constantly around the guilt I felt for lying to the *bean nighe*, getting our home destroyed, and endangering my sisters.

Oh, how I missed my room in the massive great hall on the sixth floor of the castle. I missed it all—the huge fireplace, the broken door, Finbar's roost atop the broken door, the walls covered in hair, straw,

and ancient blood.

"Hello?" The voice was gentle, and I knew who it was without looking up.

"Come in," I mumbled, still rubbing my back.

Fenora entered, a bright bouquet of flowers in her hands and another tray of food balanced on her hip. Her cheeks were bright, as if she'd been outside in the morning chill. She looked beautiful, and I resented her for it.

"I picked these this morning," she said shyly as she set the tray down beside the empty one.

I stared at the blooms. The pop of beauty in this dank place was mesmerizing. Finally, I pulled my gaze from them and looked at this strange girl. "How nice it must be," I said softly.

She tilted her head at me. "How nice what must be?"

"Being free to go about as you please. Picking flowers."

She pursed her lips, as if to consider. At long last, she smiled. "Yes, it is rather nice, isn't it? Though I would think it a great deal nicer to roam freely outside Cruachan. Tell me, how is that?"

She said it rather sharply, as though she'd just bested me in an argument. I gaped at her.

"Do you mean to say you aren't allowed to leave this place?"

"Precisely," she said. "If you're me. Others come and go as they please."

"But . . ." My mouth hung limply open. Was this girl a prisoner too? Her mother was the queen. What sort of Irish city had royalty, much less the type to keep their family prisoner? "What is this place?" I breathed.

Fenora laughed thinly. "The capital of Connacht."

I rolled my eyes. "Yes, I've heard that before. But what does that mean? Have I gone back in time or something?"

Fenora seemed to regard me thoughtfully for a few agonizing moments. "Not quite," she said at long last. "You've merely traveled outside it."

My eyebrows shot up. "What does that mean?"

She came farther into the room and seemed to consider sitting on the floor before thinking better of it and going to stand near the barred wall. "Cruachan exists outside of ordinary time. It's been here for centuries, and so have we, waiting patiently for my mother's rule."

"Ah, there's that word again," I said, gulping down a lump in my throat. "You and your mother certainly like the word 'centuries,' don't you?"

"And you like to ask an awful lot of questions," Fenora said with a smirk.

"Are you trying to tell me that this entire city has existed for centuries, you people living here, never dying, for hundreds of years? Right in the middle of Ireland?"

Fenora frowned at me, her lips settling into a soft pout that seemed to fit there naturally. Like it was her normal state of being. "People die all the time. You saw that with your own eyes only the other day."

The sight of the guards slumped on the floor, bloody swords held above them, flashed through my mind.

"We're not mortal, but we're not invincible," Fenora said with a shrug. "If that were the case, my mother wouldn't need quite so many guards."

"How old are you?" I asked.

"Only people who have been conditioned to deny the natural state of things, to deny the *sidhe*, would ask that."

The *sidhe*. The faerie people of Irish legend who lived in the hills. Ríona used to go on about them from stories in her books. But I was afraid to press Fenora any further now. If she claimed to be centuries old, which I was pretty sure she was implying, I would be forced to make a decision: to believe this nonsense she was saying and give myself over to the unreal, or to stubbornly resist the lies and commit to holding on to reality while trapped in a very real prison.

The sunshine filtering onto the floor through the bars drew me to it. Outside, a few people moved about the street, as normal as anything, as though it were still common to use horses and donkeys to pull carts along dirt roads. "So, it's just a little conclave of people interbreeding here in this city for ages?"

Fenora scoffed, drawing my gaze to her. I was standing just beside her. It startled me to see her up close, her sharp blue eyes, her skin pale and flawless. "I told you, we exist outside time. People live and die here like anywhere else. They're free to come and go. But you wouldn't understand. You've obviously given yourself over to the modern world, where people have forgotten the power of the earth and happily refuse to see things right in front of them."

I rolled my eyes, about to make a smart retort when she folded her arms across her chest and said, "You might find it strange here, but you're the same, you know."

I met her gaze, and the challenge there was clear as day. She wanted me to ask. To have to make the choice: to embrace the unreal or to keep my wits about me. "The same as what?"

"Us. You aren't of that world out there, outside Cruachan."

"Come again?" My heart was beginning to jog in my chest. It wasn't that I believed her—or understood anything this girl was saying. But I couldn't deny that there was something different about me and Ríona and Moira. There always had been.

And if this strange girl claimed to have answers, I realized with a nauseous tilt to my stomach, it was probably in my best interest to listen. Whether they were plausible or not.

"I don't know everything," she said, her powerful gaze falling to the floor at last. It felt like my own was finally free, and I turned toward my small hay bed to take a deep breath. "But you're a powerful soul," she added. "I know that much."

When I looked back, her cheeks were red, and her eyes flitted toward the door, as if she were unsure she should be saying these things.

"If I'm so powerful, why am I trapped down here?" I asked desperately.

Fenora shook her head, the beautiful frown back on her face. "That's precisely why you're here."

slán arís

ANOTHER GOODBYE

ríona

The old woman wasn't in the room with us, but it sure felt like she was. Her aura lingered among us, a ghost imprinted upon our collective memory. I knew I wasn't the only one who felt it. Each of my companions' auras quivered, a tiny aftereffect of being spooked.

Had my sisters been here to bolster me, I would have asked the question heavy on my mind: Do you think it's true? Are we the Morrigan?

For all we knew of our past, we could be. And the *bean nighe* had said . . .

But my sisters weren't there, and though I could have posed the question to Aidan, it felt like an intrusion. He was going through something as well, something I didn't quite understand. And inserting myself into the conversation wasn't something I wanted to do.

It wasn't something I ever did.

We sat in the small yellow kitchen of the cottage where Rory and Cora lived. Where their father had died. Where the legend of the selkie lived and breathed daily. A legend made flesh.

Was I one of those too? A legend in the flesh?

The tiny golden sparks that swirled around Aidan and Rory were so distinct, so distracting, I almost didn't notice how down Cora felt. The baby was asleep, tuckered out from an adventure to the babysitter's. And Cora felt anguished. Not triumphant, as she had seemed at Biddy's house, that her idea had led us somewhere, even if we weren't quite sure where that was. No, now she looked sad.

Her eyes kept flicking between Aidan and Rory, as though she too could see the sparks.

And I didn't have to wonder why for very long.

"What now, Aido?" Rory asked at long last, breaking the silence in the little kitchen.

Aidan shrugged.

"Will you stay?" Rory asked, and the desperation in his voice, the way both the human and the animal energies in him shivered, the sparks dulling, made me drop my eyes. I didn't want to see, to feel this conversation. It felt private.

"I, uh, I don't think I can," Aidan said, and his gaze skittered sideways to me. "I think you know that."

Rory nodded once, studying the scratched surface of the old wooden table. "Yeah, I figured as much. You've always been one to be off and about in the world, haven't you?"

Aidan scoffed. "Says the brother who ran off to Ireland when I needed him most." There was no rancor behind the words, and Aidan smiled to soften them, but a little hurt peeked through. "That's what kicked off all this, isn't it?"

Rory didn't say anything.

"I'll come back," Aidan said. "I promise you that. But I have to see this through." My heart leapt for Moira, even as it hurt for Aidan's family.

He glanced at me then, and our eyes met. I felt the weight of his expectations on me. If he was going to leave his family to help us, I had to step up too. Start facing our situation head-on instead of sidestepping questions about the Morrigan.

"We have to see this through," he repeated. "Whatever this is."

Silence descended on the kitchen again, and I felt compelled to contribute something. After all, I was the reason Aidan was leaving his family behind *again*. Well, me and my sisters. I had an inkling Moira had more than a little to do with it. But my borrowed pen hovered over my notepad with no conviction. I ran a finger over the small County Galway flag emblazoned on the cover of the notepad. What could I say?

My attention drifted to Cora, and I felt the hurt there, a thick fog creeping into my lungs. She seemed to be embracing the inevitability of it all. What was it like to love, to build a life, a family, with someone who'd had half his heart at sea for a decade?

As I watched, Cora lifted her eyes to Rory, who didn't meet her gaze. She looked at Aidan. "You heard what Biddy said?"

Aidan nodded once, and Rory rubbed his forehead.

I didn't have to ask what they were talking about. Biddy's last words to Aidan had left their mark on my memory too:

You must find the Macha and ask for her healing powers. Your illness runs deeper than that gash on your leg.

Did he feel it? His illness returning? And who was Macha? If these people after us thought I was the Morrigu . . . was Moira or Bríd this Macha?

"I heard," Aidan said quietly. His animal and human auras were twirling together, two dolphins leaping around one another. He glanced at Rory, who radiated pain as strongly as if he'd had a physical injury. "Stop looking at me like that," Aidan snapped. "I feel fine. I mean, except for the leg. But the rest of me—I feel better than before."

Rory nodded. "Stay the night tonight, rest up, and then go off to do whatever it is you have to do. Save the world or whatever. And then come back to us, Aido."

"I will," Aidan said firmly. "I promise I'll come back. You have to trust me. I mean, I did it once, didn't I?"

Rory's brown eyes shone warmly on his brother. "Yes, you did. Just don't take a decade this time."

don ghrá

FOR LOVE

fenora

The butterfly was a perfect specimen. It fit in the palm of my hand—but only just. It must have perished quite recently, for each fiber of its wings was still intact.

I held my palm carefully as I stepped inside the dark corridor at the back of Ráth Cruachan. If I looked at the butterfly close enough, it seemed like maybe the poor thing's wings were trembling. Like there was just a bit of life left in them.

And it was hard to accept that those wings were lifeless. They were a brilliant blue, with silver curlicues tracing the edges, nearly like the ancient carved stones on the passage tombs at the edge of Cruachan. I couldn't wait to show it to Bríd. I'd probably find her meditating down there, standing silently on one leg, one eye closed, as strange and stunning as the thin gray herons that sometimes appeared on the edges of Cruachan in search of a place to nest.

"You scurrying off to the cages again?"

I jumped, and the butterfly slipped from my palm. I drew in a sharp breath as I watched it fold in two. Those lacy silk fibers wouldn't survive the pressure of being picked up again. But I couldn't kneel to scamper all over the floor now anyway.

Pressing my lips firmly together, I turned to face my mother.

Medb stood before me, her hands clasped behind her and a cruel smile at her lips. One eyebrow lifted imperiously above me.

"I found a perfectly preserved dead butterfly," I said dumbly, trying to avoid the question.

"Well, notify the bard. We must record the occasion."

When I failed to respond, she raised her voice. "I asked what you are doing going down to the cages again."

She hadn't actually asked that, but pointing that out was not something that would benefit my well-being.

"Tell me why," she said.

Why? Maybe because having someone to speak with who wasn't Queen Medb or a brother named Maine was a dream come true. Maybe because that someone knew even less than me. Maybe because it felt fantastic to not be the lowest-ranking person on Ráth Cruachan.

"Because she's lonely," I said instead.

Medb laughed. "Good." She stared at me a moment longer before turning back toward her rooms, her skirts whirling around her.

She paused a moment, her foot in midair, and I wondered what more she had to say to me.

Until I saw it. The silky blue butterfly on the ground beneath her bare foot. She dropped her foot, ground her heel into the floor, and strode away.

In her wake was a delicate blue patch of fine threads. The ice in my chest solidified a little more, and it caused me to call out. "Mother!"

She didn't pause.

"My queen," I amended.

She stopped walking but didn't turn.

"What do you plan to do with the girl?"

That made her turn and look at me carefully. Like I'd accidentally said something intelligent.

"I'm not going to do anything," Medb said simply.

The ice got colder. "Then why . . . why keep her here?"

The grin that drew across her face couldn't really be called a smile. It was more cunning and threatening than a smile had any right to be. And it only grew more menacing as she walked back toward me. "I know you wouldn't understand it, *a leanbh*," she said, cocking her head just a fraction. Her black hair fell over her shoulder and she reached out to take a strand of my hair between her fingers. "Not having a sister, or friends, or anyone at all. It must be hard for you to imagine what one would do for someone they love." She dropped my hair and took a deep breath. "But you'll witness it soon enough."

She turned and was gone in a whirl of furs before I could tell her she was wrong. I could imagine what you would do for someone you loved. I imagined it every day. I didn't *know*, that was true enough. But I could imagine.

na bandéithe
THE GODDESSES

m o i r a

The hours were never-ending. We said little to each other, but Louis's mere presence made me angry. No matter how often he protested that he was on our side, he had so many secrets. And still he called her "queen."

Queen of what? I thought miserably, turning around to pace back toward our campsite. We hadn't moved from the spot where Ríona and Aidan had left us. I walked in circles round the place, just to get away from Louis. And to get away from my feelings of worthlessness. If we were truly these sisters of lore, these magical beings, why couldn't I *do* anything? If the curios had been our doing all along, as Louis suspected, why was the ground around me littered with nothing but sticks and dirt and rocks and not something useful, something like . . . I let loose a roar of frustration and kicked the nearest tree. I couldn't even *think* of something that might be useful right now. Except maybe

my favorite magic antlers back at home.

They'd be ash now.

At my heels, Faolan twisted his head at me. He was sluggish today and growling at shadows, treading behind me like a spooked shadow. He found me a poor substitute for Ríona.

"I couldn't agree more," I mumbled at him as the campsite came back into view. Leave it to the Girl Marked by the Blood Omen to be completely useless. I was frustrated, but my stomach still lurched at the thought of an ancient omen foretelling my death. I tried to keep it out of my mind, as anyone would, but sometimes a feeling came creeping along the back of my neck—a feeling that I was marked, destined for danger. But weren't we all?

And here Louis and I were, a pair of useless lumps just waiting for our scouting party to come back. It made me uneasy. There was nothing I could do to protect my sisters from here. I swiped at a vine hanging in my way, but it was tougher than it looked, and my wrist came away with a scrape. *What are you doing here? Just go after them!*

Maybe I should, I thought. *To hell with what Louis says. Maybe—*

Faolan tore away from me with a deep howl, making me gasp. Heart thundering, I ran after him. Exploding into the campsite, I found Louis, Conry, and Bó exactly where I'd left them. But they weren't alone.

Ríona was clinging to a very excited Faolan. As soon as she saw me, before I could even register my relief, she was on her feet and flying toward me. She wrapped me in a tight hug, infusing my body with warmth.

"Thank God you're safe," I breathed into her hair.

Faolan wound round her legs, and she released me to bend toward him again. He nuzzled his snout into her palm as she scratched him in all his favorite places. Behind them, Aidan stood awkwardly, watching our little reunion. His big brown eyes shone with warmth.

Walking quickly over to him before I lost my nerve, I wrapped my arms around him and kissed him softly on the lips. Pulling away, I murmured, "I'm glad you're okay too."

Aidan's smile was surprised but pleased. He grabbed my hand and let out a quick breath. "Better than okay. We learned some stuff, Moira."

Ríona took my hand and guided me to sit beside her. We made a little circle around the sooty mark in the grass that used to be a fire. Louis and I hadn't even attempted to keep it lit overnight.

"What did you learn?" I asked, glancing at Louis. He was wide-eyed and eager. Something in me softened. He truly looked as eager as I felt.

With a big smile, Ríona launched into ISL. *"Aidan's brother and sister-in-law introduced us to a* bean feasa," she signed.

"A *bean feasa*?" I asked aloud.

"They saw a *bean feasa*?" Louis repeated.

"A witch," Aidan supplied.

Ríona glared at him and signed, *"She is not a witch."* Aidan raised his eyebrows and looked away, as though he knew what she was reprimanding him about. Either Aidan had been studying ISL, or these two had been spending too much time together.

"Definitely a hoarder, though," Aidan grumbled.

"Okay, okay," I said, interrupting. *"Abeg!* Get to the point. Witch or not, what did she tell you?"

"The wise-woman," Ríona signed, *"she's supposed to be able to see the*

future. She even knew Aidan and his brother were selkies without having to ask. She could smell *the sea on him."*

"She could smell the sea on Aidan?" I repeated, half interpreting for the boys, half not caring whether they were part of the conversation or not.

"And then she looked at me and said I *had something strange inside me,"* Ríona signed. *"So I asked her if she'd ever heard of the Morrigan."*

"And?" I demanded. "Did she know what the Morrigan was?"

"The Morrigan is a goddess," Ríona explained. *"A goddess of old Ireland. Nobody knows if she was real or not, but it's believed she had some sort of power over kings and armies."*

"Okay," I said. "But why do they think you're her?"

"Not just me," Ríona signed. She nodded at me.

I stared at each of them in turn. "What?"

"What's she saying?" Louis asked. We ignored him.

"The Morrigan is a three-person deity," Ríona signed. *"The Morrigu is only one part of the Morrigan. She's supposed to have the power to make kings. But the other two are Badb and Macha. Badb is a goddess of battle, and Macha a goddess of the land. She's supposed to have healing powers."*

At this, Ríona glanced at Aidan, but his eyes were on the ground. They didn't say anything else. I felt like I couldn't get enough air into my lungs. "But does that make me . . . this . . . this . . ."

"Macha or Badb," Ríona finished the thought that I couldn't.

Quietly, Aidan caught Louis up on the part of the conversation he'd missed, but I found I couldn't follow it again. My thoughts were racing. People thought Ríona was the Morrigu. Did that really make me . . .

"But that's not all," Aidan added. "The Morrigan and Medb come from the same place. A place called Cruachan. It's an old city in County Roscommon. People think the Tuatha de Daanan are still there."

"The what?" I repeated.

"The *sidhe*," Louis said, a broad smile on his face. "The gods of old. Ye did it." He held up his forearm. "You got around the triskele."

"So that's correct?" I asked, feeling like I was ten steps behind everyone. "That's where Medb is? That's where they've taken Bríd?"

"What about your dad, Ríona?" Louis asked, ignoring my question. "Did they know where he might be?"

Ríona shook her head.

"We haven't really learned anything new that will help there," Aidan admitted.

"Unless Medb has him," I said, my heart racing.

"What would she want with your father?" Louis asked.

I shrug. "It's another way to get to us, *abi*? To get to Ríona? I mean, it worked, didn't it?"

"Not yet," Louis pointed out. As the excitement waned, I could see the logic returning to him. His face showed plainly that he was strategizing, calculating, trying to figure out the best thing to do next. The best thing for him, anyway.

"Well, we have to go, don't we?" Aidan said, squeezing my hand. It sent a thrill through my heart. "To Cruachan. To see if that's where Bríd has been taken."

"That's asking for death," Louis said firmly. Conry sat up and sniffed, as if he, too, knew better than us. "We have to think on this a little longer."

"No," I said, standing. "We've tried to do it your way. Now we do it ours. We're going to Cruachan."

an banphríonsa uaigneach
THE LONELY PRINCESS

bríd

Fenora came to my cell every day, and every night, Finbar came to the door. It was like having a pair of two curious little birds, each flighty and strange in their own way, both bestowing me with small gifts. Finny would come, a shiny new button in his beak, or a withered dragonfly. Then Fenora would arrive, always with a tray of food, but maybe a cup of milk and honey too, smuggled from the kitchen, she'd say, or a thick blanket of wool, or a freshly picked basket of berries.

As if any of that could make up for keeping me in a dank cell.

Each morning, I woke up with bruises, depending on how high I'd levitated in my sleep and how far I fell, but I found I didn't mind so much. Though I levitated still, I no longer dreamed of Moira's death, or Aidan betraying her. I only dreamed of our father. And I was angry enough with him that I didn't feel guilty for it.

Fenora often wore her golden hair in a braid circled around the top

of her head. I thought it looked rather like a crown and told her as much one evening, when she held out a small green plant with bare brown roots. "I feel a bit special, receiving a gift from royalty, j'know?" I said, taking the plant and giving it a dubious look. "Though I don't have any pottery on hand to give this a home, thank you for thinking of sprucing up my space."

Fenora snickered. "It's a bit of bog asphodel. Her yellow flowers are coming out now. I thought we could plant it just outside of the bars," she explained, gingerly taking the plant back from me. She stalked to the barred wall, and Finbar hopped out of sight.

He always waited until I was alone to make his presence known. Of course, the only other person who was ever in my cell was Fenora. And, I decided, she was harmless enough.

"Do you want to meet someone?" I asked, joining Fenora at the window.

She'd reached her hands through the bars and was scrabbling in the dirt outside, making a little hole for the plant.

Raising her eyebrows, she turned to me. There was something like fear in her eyes.

"Don't worry," I said, threading an arm through the bars, "he doesn't bite. *Oya*. Finny, come here."

Finbar peeked around the edge of the wall and cocked his head at me for a moment, as if to make certain I knew what I was doing, before hopping across the dirt and climbing onto my outstretched finger.

Fenora stared at Finbar. After a few moments, she cleared her throat and forced a smile onto her face. "You've been in Cruachan mere days and you've already made friends with a crow?"

I scoffed. "Jaysus, no! This is Finbar, and he and I go back very far indeed." Finbar was being awfully quiet, as he sometimes was around strangers. "Besides," I added, "the locals aren't very feckin' friendly, as you may have noticed. So I've had to bring my own friends from home."

I stuck my other arm through the bars to give Finny a scratch. He was just a fraction too big to fit through the bars, a conclusion we'd come to after much squeezing and squawking one night.

"And you're not the only one who brings me things, like," I added. A single rough-hewn bead was in Finbar's beak, and he dumped it into my palm in order to squawk, "Things. Things. Things."

"I see that," Fenora said, real amusement slowly replacing the strange forced smile on her face. She tucked a stray lock of hair behind her ear and went back to her task in the dirt. When she'd finished, she brushed her palms off and stuck a finger out. "Will he come to me?"

Finbar assessed her finger with one beady eye.

"He's a bit timid," I said. "He's not sure he likes you yet." Finbar leaned into the pressure of my thumb. "Go on, Finny. Go say *hi*. In spite of it all, it seems like she might be all right."

When I looked up, Fenora was watching me intently. Seriously. Like I was a complicated riddle that needed solving. She jumped a little when Finbar hopped onto her finger, which was still outstretched, a forgotten invitation.

"It tickles, doesn't it?" I asked.

Fenora giggled, one of the first signs of lightheartedness I'd heard from her. "Just a little." She looked uncomfortable, like she wasn't sure what to do with her body.

"You needn't be so stiff," I said. "He won't fall off, like."

"Fall off!" Finbar screeched.

"Oh," Fenora said, going even more stiff. "I . . . I'm not good with animals."

"Really?" I asked. "How's that possible? There are so many here." As we spoke, cattle and sheep made themselves heard on a nearby road.

"Yes, for farming," Fenora said. "But not . . . pets."

"Well, Finny won't thank you for calling him a pet. He's a companion. But have you never had a dog, or even a cat that comes round your house every now and again looking for food?"

"No," Fenora said, her eyes darting between me and Finny, like she couldn't decide who was more interesting to look at.

"No, no, no," Finbar sang.

"That's feckin' tragic," I said, folding my arms over my chest and slumping against the wall. "My sisters and I each have our own animal companions. A girl can't ever fully quench loneliness without an animal who knows her heart."

Fenora swallowed. "I'd believe that."

She said it with such gravity, such sadness. But a resigned sadness, the kind that has had time to solidify inside you and ice over anew each day. Did this girl have no one but her coldhearted mother to be with? And maybe those sharp-chinned men she'd been standing with behind her mother's throne?

The minute I recognized my next thought, I felt guilty, but the thought stayed with me: maybe this lonely girl held the answer to finding a way out of here.

"Would your mother not allow you an animal?" I asked carefully, afraid she'd shy from the topic of her mother. "Does she not like animals?"

Fenora shifted her weight from one foot to the other, careful not to jostle Finbar, like he was made of glass and would topple from her finger if she moved too much. "Medb doesn't like much of anything," she said. "At least she hasn't in quite a long time."

That was a strange thing to say about one's mother. Memories of walking down the rustyback hill to the sea, hand-in-hand with my own mother and one of my sisters, flooded my brain. I closed my eyes against the onslaught. I knew not everyone had a mother as wonderful as mine. After all, this girl's mother had no problem hunting down helpless teenagers and imprisoning the innocent.

"It's not entirely her fault," Fenora went on. "It's just who she is that's the problem. No one in Cruachan would come within a hundred yards of Medb's daughter if they could help it. Sometimes I can *see* people inching away from me, trying to put just a little more space between us, like they can't even help it. It's just a self-preservation instinct."

"Are they scared of you?" I asked. I couldn't imagine anyone being scared of this soft golden girl who'd just planted a bog asphodel outside my window and actually knew what a bog asphodel was.

"No," she said thoughtfully as she mimicked the way I stroked Finbar's inky black head. "They're scared of her. They don't know me well enough to know I'm not like her."

Not like her. The words hung heavy in my chest. The problem was, I didn't think she was like Medb. Not in my heart. But I also knew it would be awfully naive to come to that conclusion so easily.

"Well, you'll be the queen after her," I said calmly. "It's in their best interests to be careful, j'know?"

Fenora shook her head. "Anyone with sense knows there is no queen after Medb."

That sounded quite fatalistic, and I felt bad for her, but I was distracted too. My heart was beating faster, the wind inside my chest picking up, eager to see just how long this girl would talk. It was on the tip of my tongue to ask her what her mother wanted with me and my sisters, when she went on:

"Whenever I do speak with someone who's gotten close, some lad who's come round because he wants to get near my mother—because there are the brave ones, you know. The conniving ones. The ones with schemes. Well, they just end up finding me . . . strange."

"It's not such a bad thing to be strange," I said, nodding at Finny. "Like having a crow for a best friend." *And feeling the wind alive inside you. And dreaming things that have yet to come true.*

Fenora smiled. "That's not strange. That's lovely."

My heart was taking flight, and I could feel the urge to show this girl just what strange could mean. In the hope that she would share too. At least, that was what I told myself. If I shared my secrets, maybe she would share hers. But more than that, I wanted to be known. Truly, honestly known. I always did. Wasn't that why I'd shared our secrets with Louis back in Bunrowan in the first place? And look how that had turned out. I'd thought he'd been head over heels for me before catching him shifting my sister.

Leave it to Bríd to make the same mistake twice, Moira would say.

But my mind was working through the same equation over and

over again, without coming to any conclusion: *If Ríona is the Morrigu, and I'm Badb, that makes Moira this Macha. The sisters three.*

My brain couldn't stay in that loop forever, adding no new information or insight. I needed to let somebody else in.

"Can you keep a secret?" I asked.

Fenora cocked her head. "I wouldn't know. I have no one to keep secrets for."

Her honesty threw me off-balance. "Well, I guess that's good enough for me. My sisters and I . . . we are quite strange, like. That must be why your mother thinks we're the Morrigan . . . the 'sisters three.' Strange things happen around us. And I . . . I dream things."

"That's not so strange," Fenora said. "Doesn't everyone dream?"

I was nearly scared to go on, not sure making this admission would get her to reveal anything important in return. And what if she told Medb? The queen already suspected something strange of me and my sisters, but how much did she really know? Wouldn't this knowledge just make her more resolute in her suspicions of us? The wind in my chest wouldn't die down. Somehow, I knew it wouldn't rest until the words, the truth, was out. "Yes, but . . . my dreams come true."

Fenora quirked her eyebrows. "Do you mean . . . ?"

"I have visions of the future," I finished for her.

Fenora wasn't looking at me anymore. She was staring at Finbar.

"Do you think it's true?" I prodded. "That my sisters and I . . . that we are . . . *them?*"

Finally, Fenora looked at me. And she didn't say anything for a long time. Just stared, her lips parted, her breathing steady. "I don't know," she said at last.

And for the first time since I'd met her, I had the impression she wasn't telling me the truth. The whole truth, anyway. I glanced at her wrist but saw nothing like Louis's triskele. No, this girl's duplicity was all natural.

"Why do you come to see me?" I asked. "Does your mother make you?"

This time, the truth was plain on her face. "No."

Her motive was loneliness, plain and simple. "How can royalty be so lonely?" I murmured.

Fenora smiled weakly. "I don't know. But I'm not lonely right now."

níos mó ná dualgais
MORE THAN DUTY

m e d b

The look on her face as she climbed the stairs was euphoric. I knew where she'd been. Her golden hair and pale skin, the way her mouth naturally turned down at the edges, like she was thinking hard, it still made my stomach flip with the shadow of nausea, a half-remembered grief.

Her frown. Her blue eyes. Her golden hair. Findabair was her father's daughter, not mine. The boys, they were mine, clear enough. If it wasn't the dark hair, it was the cold smile, the easy confidence, that marked every one of them as mine.

But Findabair ... at various times over the decades, I had wondered if it was somehow his infidelity and a dark magic that had placed her in my womb. But no, every now and again, she said something cunning or smiled at a frivolous boy in such a crooked,

masterful way that I knew she was mine after all. She was the blood of my blood and the flesh of my flesh. At the very core, she was the daughter of Medb.

And right now, her perpetual frown was tilted upward on one side, like it was fighting the inevitable transformation into something akin to happiness. I couldn't believe I hadn't seen it before.

My strategy had been flawed from the outset. I had something much stronger than old dusty blackmail in my possession. I would take advantage of something more potent than duty.

It may have been luck—and the failure of useless men—that had put a broken daughter of Morrigan into my hands. But when luck was wielded by a master, victory was sure.

And I was a master.

No, I was better than that. I was a queen.

baile átha cliath
DUBLIN

louis

"We will be butchered!" I yelled for the third time. Conry let out a howl. The others jumped. But I was too angry to quiet Conry. We were hiding out in a copse in the east of County Galway. I kept us moving, our campsite changing as much as possible, and that, at least, the others agreed to. Our next step, however, was hotly contested.

"We have heard your opinion, thank you," Moira snapped. Bó stamped a foot and turned away from us, done with the noise. The mare was as temperamental and stubborn as her girl.

"Moira, wait," Aidan said, a hand on her arm. "We have to listen to him. He's the only one of us who knows what we're walking into."

"But we can't trust him! Who knows what he really wants to happen?"

Ríona signed furiously at her sister, which only made Moira groan and throw her hands up. Ríona peeked at me shyly, and I wondered if it

had been a defense of me she'd been communicating. The selkie defending me had been surprise enough.

"Moira, I know it's scary," Aidan said, a hand on each of her shoulders. He stumbled a bit when he put too much weight on his injured leg. "But we have to trust him. We have no other option right now."

"But he can't even tell us anything," Moira snapped, gesturing toward the triskele on my forearm. "Or he *won't.*"

I looked from Ríona to Moira to Aidan, willing them to believe me. "I *can't.*"

We stood around, avoiding each other's eyes. Each of us alone in our fear.

We had to go to Cruachan; I knew that. But that was precisely what Medb wanted at the moment. Walking right into her hands wouldn't help anyone. How could I make Moira see that?

Still, I didn't have a better plan. Unless . . .

"There might be someone who can help," I said carefully, testing the boundaries of the triskele.

Moira rounded on me, full of fury. Her love for her sisters, her protection of them, was scary sometimes. "You just thought of someone?" she asked, her eyes narrowed. "How on Earth are we supposed to believe that?"

I clenched my hands. "This whole not-trusting-me thing is getting truly old."

"Forgive me for not believing every absurd thing you say," Moira grumbled, clearly not seeking forgiveness at all.

I thought about telling them then. Telling them who I was,

launching into it, triskele side effects be damned. Looking down at my wrist, I remembered the pain. When Moira had made me use the truth pen back at the castle to tell my secrets, Medb's secrets, the triskele had glowed red, and my arm had burned like it had been thrust into the heart of a fire. That pain had lanced straight through my body to my inner being. It was like being stabbed with a glowing iron. What fate had Medb woven into the triskele? What would happen if I tried to speak through the pain?

Moira's huff of annoyance brought me back to myself. If they didn't believe what they knew so far, what would make them believe I was a god of old?

No, that story would have to wait. Right now, we had to save their sister from Medb. Or they would never trust me again. Ríona stood beside me, fidgeting with the fur on Faolan's back. What I wouldn't have given for a peek inside her head.

Her gaze was on the ground, and just before I looked away, she raised her eyes and looked at me straight on.

When I'd first met her at the castle, those eyes had been full of temerity and uncertainty. Now? Now she held my gaze, not smiling, not frowning, just seeing, until I broke away.

"Well?" Moira snapped. "*Abeg*, convince me I should believe you."

Ríona reached out and took her sister's hand. Moira looked at her for a long, quiet moment. They stood like that so long, communicating without words, that I was sure our conversation was over. But finally, Moira turned back to me.

"I will listen to you," she said, practically glaring. "But that is all I can promise right now. Whether we do it your way or my way, we are going to Cruachan to save our sister."

"I agree," I said. "All I ask is that we make one stop first."

"Where?" Moira demanded.

I studied each of my companions in turn. Aidan looked desperate, Ríona hopeful, Moira . . . furious. I took a deep breath. "Dublin."

eolas na déithe

WHAT THE GODS KNOW

bríd

I'd been lying in my bed all morning, waiting for Fenora, dozing in and out of consciousness, when the door to my cell swung open. "Jaysus, finally!" I mumbled, rolling over to greet her.

Fenora stood just inside the door. And before her, slowly taking in each musty corner of my little cave, was her mother.

I jumped to my feet.

We stared at each other in silence. Fenora wouldn't meet my eyes. She wouldn't even look up from the floor. Was her mother here because of what I'd told Fenora, about my dreams, my visions?

"I trust you're well?" Medb said at long last. Her gaze felt like a heavy weight on my shoulders. Though the words were the kind to be spoken out of polite interest, the coldness in her eyes was unmistakable. I wanted nothing more than to crawl through the bars of the cell and follow Finbar into the sky. Far, far away from here.

Medb raised her eyebrows at me, her impatience clear.

"I-I'm fine."

Medb nodded. "Now, let's speak plainly. Your family has something I need, and yet you know very little about it. Meanwhile, your father has betrayed your family and left you in danger. Your destruction isn't my wish, nor should my failure be yours. We are not enemies, Badb." She clasped her hands in front of her, tilting her head a fraction, as though I were a curious specimen she studied. "Do you understand?"

It felt like . . . a test of some sort. But I had no idea how to pass, what I should say—or what she wanted me to say. I knew what I wanted to say: *Don't call me that! I am not her! I'm not a feckin' goddess!*

But I knew that wouldn't get me anywhere. The things I'd told Fenora had likely only solidified Medb's insistence that my sisters and I were the "sisters three" she'd spoken of. The Morrigan. But my brain was in survival mode, and I didn't care what she thought at the moment—or what I thought. I just wanted to give her the words she wanted to hear in order to get myself out of this place. But I couldn't imagine what those magic words might be.

All my muddled brain could come up with was: "Okay."

It came out soft and weak, a true coward's plea.

Without another word, Medb turned to leave, gesturing for Fenora to precede her. Fenora twirled on the spot and scurried out the door. Medb gave me one last imperious look, picked up the skirt of her moss-green dress, and stepped through the doorway.

Leaving the door open.

I gaped after her.

The queen paused on the other side of the threshold and turned her head, speaking over her shoulder. "Are you coming? I won't stay down here all day waiting."

Without a single thought, I ran after her.

MEDB didn't stop walking, never turned to see if I was following. Even when Fenora paused at the foot of the stairs to the mound, bowed toward her mother, and turned to disappear into the busy street, Medb kept moving. I didn't stop, either.

She led me up the stairs, into the throne room, and straight through it. On the other side of a low doorway, we came to a smaller, dimly lit room stuffed full of furniture draped in animal skins. There were no people here, but the air was close with the heat of a fire in the hearth.

Beyond this, there were kitchens, full of people who stopped to stare. Almost a dozen pairs of eyes on us. But Medb didn't acknowledge any of them, just moved onward to a door outside. I'd never been this way and didn't know what lay at the back of the house.

Medb paused beneath the lintel. Sunlight fell across half her face, making it appear more menacing than ever. "You will be housed near the other young girls, and I shall show you to a place where you can wash momentarily. But first, I would like to show you something."

She turned to continue outside. This sudden change from prisoner in a dark cell to the freedom of the outside world was making me shaky and unsure. "Wh-What do you want from me?" I spoke up, feeling my legs tremble. "Why am I no longer a prisoner?"

Medb regarded me a moment, her face still in that half-light.

Behind me, the sounds of a busy kitchen slowly started up again, as if the people there were trying not to eavesdrop. "You are being released to live in my court because my daughter speaks highly of you. And I think highly of my daughter."

I considered challenging that. I hadn't seen any evidence of Medb thinking highly of anyone. But I was in unknown territory already. Instead, I asked, "But . . . what about my family? All that you said about my family and my dad?"

Medb smiled ruefully, kicked off her slippers, and walked through the door. "You have much to learn, *a leanbh*. Come along."

Just outside the door was a wild garden full of vegetables and blooms in various stages of growth. Tall fairy thimbles and tiny clumps of bog rosemary grew side by side. A girl in a worn dress kneeled among the pointy green tops of parsnips. She jumped up when she saw us, grabbing the basket beside her and shuffling back inside as fast as she could.

"Do you hear them?" Medb said, opening her palms toward the sky.

The sounds of the city down at the bottom of the mound came to me. One could see for miles from up here. The town was bustling and busy, and I took in the sight of it all for a moment. Far off, I could see the edges of the city, and the empty land beyond, fields dotted only by livestock and the shadows of birds. I was transfixed.

Until I realized I *did* hear it. A buzzing. Laid over the background noise. It sounded like the beehive Moira had kept in an urn in the storage room back at home.

"Bees?" I asked, a feeling of danger coming over me. What she'd said about me living in her court—had that been a lie? Was she going to hurt me instead? Torture me? Eventually kill me? Had releasing me from my prison been merely a fun ruse to make me walk freely to my death? The wind whipped into a tornado in my gut, and I thought I might hurl. *No*, I told myself, *she wouldn't hurt you. She wants Ríona, and you are her best connection to her now.*

Medb seemed to float down the dirt path, light on her bare toes, to a long wooden fence at the end of it. As I came nearer, I saw this area was full of wild flowers. Bees and flying insects of all types were thick in the air, delighting in a riot of colorful flowers. But that wasn't where the buzzing came from.

Dotted among the flowers were tall closed-top baskets of woven straw. The collective noise was enough to imagine an entire hive alive inside each one.

Medb bent and reached out to touch a hand gently against the straw of the nearest basket, as though she were touching the most precious stone in the world. "Do you hear them?" she repeated.

The hum was loud and rhythmic at this close distance. "Yes," I said.

"No, I mean *hear* them," Medb said, placing a hand on her heart.

I just stared at her.

"No, you don't." After watching me a beat longer, she said, "You don't understand them at all."

She sounded . . . disappointed. As though she had higher hopes for me.

I shrugged, looking around us. I couldn't count all the hives, but at least ten stood out among the flowers closest me. "I guess I don't. Why do you keep bees?"

Medb looked at me for a long moment. "One doesn't *keep* bees," she said, stroking the basket with one long finger. "The bees keep us." With that, she lifted the basket from the ground, revealing there was no bottom to it. Bees poured out of the open end. Medb plunged her hand inside.

The humming grew to a fever pitch, but the swarm didn't hurt her. The displaced bees rose into the air and circled Medb, but she didn't flinch.

"They are the last vessel of the wisdom of the gods."

I took a wary step back as more bees descended from the sky in a vibrating funnel around Medb's arm. They cloaked her skin like a sleeve all the way up to the edge of her dress at her elbow.

"Do you know how I came to be here, *a leanbh*?" Medb asked.

I bristled at being called a child but merely shook my head. Medb didn't appear to want an answer. The bees continued to crawl along her arm, finding new spaces to fill. She dug her toes into the grass.

"Cruachan is my birthright. It was my mother's, by the grace of the gods. My mother was the handmaiden to an unfortunate *sidhe* girl who fell in love with the wrong person. The girl's punishment was rebirth. Rebirth as a mortal." The bees were climbing across her shoulders now and down her other arm. "As this *sidhe* girl's handmaiden, my mother was reborn with her, condemned to the mortal realm as well. But her mistress had known a love too strong to be broken by the magic of bitter druids. Her *sidhe* lover came for her, to take her back, and brought her maid too."

The bees crawled down Medb's body, encompassing the entire

bodice of her green dress.

"On the long journey back, they stopped at many *sidhe* mounds along the way, including here, in this hill. My mother asked if it belonged to her mistress's *sidhe* lover. It was grander than anything she'd ever seen. But it was an ignorant question. His palace was eleven times the size of this. But he knew its inhabitants well. He respected my mother for the duty she'd done his lover. And so, he gifted it to her. Named it in her honor. And when he journeyed on to his own palace with his love, my mother stayed and made this place her own. She built this hall—this hall that became the center of Cruachan. She fell in love, she birthed children, but always she ruled this land from right here on Ráth Cruachan."

"And you've been here ever since?" I asked, my stomach turning when I tried to conquer that incomprehensive concept of time.

Medb turned to me, and I gasped.

Her entire body was covered in buzzing insects—except her head. She watched me watch her. Her neck, her arms, her torso, even the folds of her skirt were ensconced. I involuntarily stumbled back a few steps, but the bees had no interest in me.

"Something like that," Medb said softly.

She dropped her eyes to her arms, which she stretched in front of her. The bees crawled and moved as if her skin were honeycomb and they were at work. My heart was in my throat. My skin prickled as though a thousand tiny insect feet crawled over *me*.

Finally, Medb said, "Did you know their entire lives are organized around a single queen?" The look on her face when she said it was as placid as if she were stating the weather. "The power of the divine feminine never ceases to amaze."

I had a feeling we weren't just talking about the bees.

After a long moment, Medb took a deep breath and whispered, "*Sínigí amach bhur gcuid sciatháin.*"

The bees lifted from her skin and swirled into the sky, dissipating in moments. Medb stood there, in a shimmering black gown.

I stared. Her dress had been transformed. Where before she'd worn a simple green shift dress, she was now covered in a black gown filled with such sparkling light as the night's sky, or the starlight reflecting off the ocean on a moonless night. It moved as though with a gentle breeze.

"Jaysus," I whispered. "Did the bees do that?"

"We have much in common, Badb," Medb said. "You may not say it, but I can sense it in you: You too yearn for what your birth promised you. But it was stolen from you. And you have spent your life waiting to get it back. The time has come for you to claim it."

I had no clear idea what she was talking about, but I also felt the truth in my bones. How many years had I sat staring out my top-floor window at Bunrowan, wishing something would happen? Something exciting. Something real. Something that made sense of everything I'd ever felt: The wind. Finbar. The dreams.

A single bee still crawled along Medb's collarbone. She stretched out a finger, and the bee crawled on to it. She lifted it high, and the bee took to the air. I watched its dizzying path until I lost it in a sunbeam.

"*Ná bíodh faitíos ort,*" Medb whispered. I did not know if she was talking to me or the lone bee. *Do not be afraid.*

saol na cúirte
A LIFE AT COURT

b r í d

My bed was in a squat wooden roundhouse on a mound they called Ráth da Dtarbh, which I came to learn was home to Fenora and a gaggle of girls our age who fussed with Fenora's hair anytime she stood still and brought her things before she asked for them.

When Medb had me escorted there, it took my eyes a moment to adjust to the dank interior, but what I found was cozier than my room in Bunrowan. The fire in the middle of the room was a warm beacon that the girls gathered around, as if its very flames gave them life. It emitted a plume of smoke that twirled lazily upward through the room to a hole in the very center of the ceiling.

The fire was the heartbeat of the house. Someone was constantly tending it, throwing another log on or yelling for someone else to do it. And each time the fire flashed, the bronze skeleton of the house gleamed in tandem with the spears and iron weapons hanging on the

wall.

That first evening out of my cell, after I'd been shown to my bed in the roundhouse and the area at the back reserved for bathing, I was retrieved by a sheepish Fenora to dine with her in the hall on An Ráth Mór, the biggest mound and building in Cruachan.

"Only if you're hungry," she'd said, not meeting my eyes.

I wondered how much she knew about her mother's plans. Did her mother confide in her? Were they in this together?

No. The look on her face told me she was just as in over her head as I was. She had probably been born in over her head. I felt myself soften toward her.

"I'm starving, like," I said.

Fenora smiled.

The giant wooden structure of An Ráth Mór was full of smoke and flame, the air thick with the scent of meat and alcohol. A huge fire was in the middle, tended by sweaty cooks who ladled out stew and threw bannocks at anyone who jostled forward for them before retreating to the wooden tables inside the hall and out. But I never had to go near the cooking fires. Anyone with Fenora needn't lift a finger.

Women appeared with food and drink for all of the girls in the princess's entourage. *I could get used to this*, I thought, lifting a metal cup of amber liquid to my lips. It was sweet, and it sent a pleasant buzz straight to my head, as if a tiny bee were making itself at home there.

"Jaysus, what is this?" I asked Fenora breathlessly.

She looked about ready to roll her eyes, but the girl next to me giggled and said, "Mead," before taking a swig from her own cup. "You know, the nectar of the gods. For divine strength."

Fenora did roll her eyes then.

The amber liquid winked up at me in the light from the fire. I took another gulp. "Is it . . . honey?"

"It's made with fermented honey," Fenora said.

Mmm. No wonder Medb kept a horde of bees on hand.

Two men appeared at our table then, both young men with sharp chins, mischievous eyes, dark hair, and insufferable smirks. I recognized them as part of the group that had stood with Fenora behind her mother's throne that very first day.

"What do *you* want?" Fenora demanded, not even looking up from her food.

A few of the other girls sat up straighter and touched nervous hands to carefully arranged hair. The men pretended not to notice, but they shared covert looks of amusement.

"We only came to introduce ourselves to our esteemed guest," the shorter of the two said.

Fenora sighed loudly, but the man ignored her and faced me. "I am Maine Máthramail, son of Medb, warrior queen of Connacht, sovereignty goddess of all Ireland, and daughter of Eochaid Feidlech, High King of Ireland."

"And I am Maine Mórgor, son of Medb, warrior queen of—"

"Yeah, I got it," I said, interrupting. "Nice to meet you. Fenora didn't mention she had brothers."

The first cocked his head. "Why doesn't that surprise me?"

"Seven of them," Fenora grumbled, glaring at a potato like it was personally responsible.

"The Maine brothers," the girl beside her said breathlessly.

"The what?" I repeated. "They're all feckin' named Maine?"

The first Maine grinned. "A druid once told my mother her son Maine would be the one to kill Conchobar of Ulster. She didn't have a son named Maine. So, we all took on the name."

I gaped at him. "She just created her own little army to trick fate? How sweet."

Fenora snorted, but the brothers were unfazed. "We do hope to see more of you, Badb," the first said, bowing his head.

"Mm-hmm," I murmured, picking up my cup of mead. When they turned and walked away, I snorted into the golden liquid. "Oh, Lord, give me the divine strength to avoid them."

Fenora laughed but nudged me in the side. "Do take it slow," she said. "You can get drunk on divine strength, you know."

Later that night, lying down and pulling the covers up over me in my new warm bed felt more comforting than anything I could remember experiencing before. I snuggled deeper under the pile of pelts.

My sisters would come for me. I knew it. Louis and Aidan would help them find me. But until then . . . well, there was no point in not enjoying the most excitement I'd experienced in my lifetime.

MEDB never joined us for meals, but she called Fenora from Ráth da Dtarbh often, and Fenora usually asked me to accompany her. Every time, I became more enamored with Cruachan. We ate fruit dipped in honey. We watched young men who dreamed of war take on Medb's sons in combat of all kinds, from spears to fists. We sat in the wildflowers and watched as Medb's servants tended to the bees. They wore long, white, hooded shifts that covered every inch of skin, along with a woven straw circle that inserted into the hood and covered the face. The effect was frightening. I loved every minute.

I learned how to repair the straw skeps that housed the hives, and then sat nearby and picked fruit out of a cup of mead while somebody else actually fixed them. Sometimes I'd simply sit on a pelt while Fenora recited the poems, stories, and knowledge that her mother insisted she learn. Fenora frowned through it all.

It was during one such visit, when we were lounging in the back garden near the bees, that I thought to ask Fenora, "Where's your father?"

We were lying on a plaid blanket spread near the middle of the garden. I was staring up at the blue sky. The other girls were moving through the flowers around us, picking the prettiest blooms to bring back to Ráth da Dtarbh, giggling and whispering about lads they knew, including those named Maine. Thankfully, they weren't paying us any attention because Fenora's face had changed just then. Her characteristic frown returned, and her tired eyes looked at the ground.

"I don't know."

"Feck, I'm sorry," I murmured. "My mam's gone too. And now my dad's missing."

It was out before I thought to consider my words. Did she already know this? Medb had claimed my father betrayed us. Did Fenora know the truth of it?

"Fenora," I said softly. "Do you . . . do you know where my dad is? What he's done?"

Fenora was silent so long I thought maybe she was trying to come up with the words to tell me. I didn't press her. "You'll have to ask my mother," she said finally.

My eyelids shut tight, squeezing away the threat of tears, and then I looked at the sky. *Finbar, where are you?*

It felt as though I could handle anything, if only I had my Finny back with me.

But no matter how often I looked, from out here in the garden, or down on the street, or at the door of Ráth da Dtarbh, I hadn't seen him since I'd been locked up. I'd even sneaked away from the roundhouse this morning in order to try to find the door to my cell from the outside. Just in case Finbar still went there in search of me. I'd found the cell, still empty, but Finbar hadn't been there. It made my stomach turn. We'd never had trouble finding each other before. Maybe he'd gone to find Ríona and Moira after all.

"*Miodh?*" It was Medb's voice. Coming up behind us. A girl scurried along at her heels, carefully balancing a tray laden with cups of mead.

I sat up and took one eagerly. Medb sat beside Fenora and tucked her legs beneath her, her feet bare. She wore a pale dress with a maroon cloak around her shoulders, clasped with an ornate silver brooch. Her dark hair fell long and wild over her shoulders.

This, I'd come to learn, was Medb's natural state.

"Fenora?" she prompted, sliding her eyes between her daughter and the girl with the tray. Fenora only shook her head. This parley between mother and daughter was getting familiar.

Medb usually had a story to share or some tidbit about Cruachan and what was happening that day. I would listen intently; Fenora would look away, barely tuned into the conversation. However, this time, Fenora faced her mother fully and asked, "Bríd asked about her father."

My mouth hung open. I hadn't been about to bring that up with Medb. Not right now. I had wanted to think about it. To come up with a plan for approaching Medb with more information. Fenora looked away, at a servant moving a bee skep.

Medb looked at me. "Strange. I didn't hear anything."

Her eyes didn't leave my face. It was as good a chance as any. "Where's my dad?" I asked, hating the way my voice broke.

Medb leaned back, releasing a deep, gratifying sigh. "The spirit of Badb grows stronger in you by the day. Embrace it."

But I didn't want to embrace it. I didn't want to be Badb. I wanted to be Bríd. Bríd Doyle.

"You know, of course, what business your father traded in," Medb said. "He was known for his deals with your magic. It was only a matter of time before he made a bad deal."

"I . . . I don't understand," I said. Dad had traveled the country selling the curios created by the castle; I knew that much. And Louis had told us that it wasn't the castle that was creating the curios at all. It was us. So, then it was a little bit true what Medb said—that Dad had been, more or less, selling our magic . . .

"He's a greedy man, your father," Medb explained. "And the little magical items he sold, they weren't enough. When someone in my court offered him a fortune for knowledge of the Morrigu's whereabouts, he gave it up easily. His soul, his daughters' safety . . . he traded it for money."

No. That wasn't what the pillow at Bunrowan had said. It had said: *And upon a day dark and dreary, at this kitchen table, did Brian Doyle sign away his soul for those of his ruthless daughters.* That meant he had traded his soul for ours. He had saved us.

I shook my head. "I think he traded something terrible to save us. Not endanger us."

"Oh?" Medb smiled, and the effect was chilling. "If that's so, why has your father forsaken you? Why did he miss your birthday?"

My head jerked up. How had she known that?

"Eighteen and coming into powers none of you understand. And he left you all alone in the world."

That's not what the pillow said, I repeated in my head, over and over again, the wind in me picking up. *Oh, Jaysus, am I going to believe a pillow above the flesh-and-blood woman before me?*

"Your father isn't coming back, Badb," Medb said. "You know it; your sisters know it. That's how we've gotten to this place. That's how you came to be here."

I covered my face with my hands, dropping them to my bent knees. I felt vaguely like I might throw up. *Keep to the castle and the castle will take care of you.* That was what Dad had always said. Only, that wasn't true, was it? We'd been attacked and driven out of the castle. We'd faced more danger than we'd seen in our entire lives. And Dad hadn't been there to protect us.

Wiping the tears from my eyes, I choked out, "I don't believe you."

"No," Medb said, almost kindly, "I don't suppose you do. And I wish, for your sake, that it were otherwise."

rí ar bhád

KING ON A BOAT

ríona

"He's a bit royal," Louis explained. Moira and I exchanged looks. How could one be "a bit" royal? The sounds of Dublin were soft, dampened by the miles and miles we'd traveled up the River Liffey to find this green-and-black monstrosity before us.

"If he's royal, why is he here?" Moira asked, frowning at the dilapidated boat. It looked as though it would sink beneath the murky river water at any moment.

"Because of you."

I stared, openmouthed. Moira made an indignant squawk. Bó gave a soft whinny and shook her head, making her bridle clang against the lamppost Moira had tied her to. Bó seemed to find this situation quite undignified.

"What is that supposed to mean?" Moira asked, bristling. She reached a hand out and splayed her fingers across Bó's flank, calming

the mare even as her own temper flared.

Louis shrugged. "Let's let him tell the tale, shall we? After all . . ." He held up his arm. The triskele was as black as night in the light of day.

Moira huffed, but there was only one way we would get to the bottom of all this. And it wasn't by standing around arguing any longer. I thought of Bríd and what she might have been doing right then. What she might have been being made to do. How I wished I could read her feelings right then.

We had no time to waste.

Taking a deep breath, I did a little run and launched myself off the quay and across the gap onto the pocked deck of the boat. It wasn't even a houseboat, by the looks of it. Just a big wooden fishing vessel with chipping green and black paint and a mess of lobster traps covering the deck. I barely missed tripping right over one.

Louis gaped at me, mouth open. Faolan was at my heels before any of the others.

"God, Ríona, you'll give me a heart attack one day," Moira muttered, tucking her hair behind her ears and stepping up to the edge. I put my hand out to help her follow me onto the deck, but Aidan was there, his split auras twirling as he leapt across before Moira and reached back for her. His injury left him unsteady, though, and he crashed to a knee as he turned, his body off off-kilter. In a flash, Moira had jumped across and bent to help him, as he grumbled and brushed off his knees. They were like that more and more—together, right where the other was, helping, touching, murmuring. The water gently knocked the boat side to side, water and boat a similar dark, mossy green. Aidan looked down at the water, and I felt his cold crash of longing. Then Moira's hand was in his, and the warm, quiet side of him wrapped thin tendrils around the other, bringing it back from the brink. Was that how Aidan lived? Always at the brink of becoming something else completely?

Without a backward glance, Louis launched himself onto the boat. His feelings, his thoughts were obscured from me. I couldn't feel them like I could other people's. And that just made me want to feel them more. Unbidden, the memory of his lips on mine came to me, the one time I had truly felt what he was feeling.

At least, I'd thought it was what he'd been genuinely feeling. If I'd asked Moira, she probably would have pointed out that that kiss could have been part of Louis's plan, whatever that might be.

The golden girl in a castle by the sea. That was all I could remember of the poem. The rest had burned with Bunrowan.

Conry let out a howl, raising the hair on the nape of my neck, and Louis called out, "Hello?" They were already at the door to the cabin near the front of the boat. The cabin was barely large enough to fit a handful of grown men at a time, and I wasn't exactly sure who Louis was expecting to find in there, but the rest of us had only made it halfway across the deck when an older man popped up in the window.

"*Cé atá ann?*" he demanded, his voice muffled in the little room.

Conry gave a big yawn before sitting down beside the door. The man was big, with mountainous shoulders, a thick neck, and a weathered, tan face. His gaze found Conry first, before moving to Louis, as if looking for him. His shoulders dropped, and a scowl twisted his craggy face.

"Well," Moira grumbled, "apparently, Louis here has enemies in more than one county in Ireland."

I threw her a stern look, but a corner of my lip picked up. The man with the wild white hair did indeed appear quite perturbed to see Louis on his boat. A foggy gray mist hung around him as he opened the door to the cabin cautiously, and I caught sight of blankets and a pillow tangled on the floor of the tiny room. It didn't look very comfortable.

The man stepped onto the deck, barefoot, and crossed his arms over his chest. The annoyance was wafting off him, a heavy cologne in the fog of his aura. "*Cù?*"

"Did he just call you a dog?" Moira asked.

"Hound," Louis said, as if the clarification was important. He didn't look away from the older man, who seemed to wilt under Louis's gaze.

Still, the man's annoyance hung heavily around him as his lined face studied each of us in turn, giving Faolan an extra-long look. "Spill it all now," he spat. "Did she send you?"

Louis looked steadily at him. "I'm bound by the triskele."

The man's eyes flitted to Louis's forearm and, finding the swirling mark there, gave a world-weary sigh. He was familiar with the triskele then.

"I'm here because we need your help." Louis nodded toward us. "They need your help."

The man glanced at us again. "And who might they be?" He and Louis both turned to us, waiting. Aidan and I both looked to Moira.

"I'm . . . I'm Moira," she said, stumbling forward. Louis gave her an exacerbated look. "What?" she added. "Sir? M'lord?" She turned to Louis. "And you? Who exactly are you?"

"Listen, you have to tell him the truth, or all of this is for naught," Louis said through gritted teeth. "We will discuss me later."

"Of course we will," Moira muttered, releasing a loud breath through her nose. I was feeling overwhelmed with everyone's collective irritation. "Well, sir, I would be happy to answer your question, only we don't know the answer ourselves. Apparently, some well-placed people believe us to be this—this three-person goddess called The Morrigan."

Moira was prepared to go on, but the man wasn't looking at her anymore. He was staring at Louis, a bright white light piercing through his annoyance. "If she didn't send you, why are you with them?"

Louis gave a little shrug. "I've been wrong before. That should be no surprise to you. Allegiances change in this world. You know that better than anyone." The man scoffed, but Louis wasn't done. "You have to help them." It was a heartfelt plea.

The man looked at Louis for a long time, the white light growing. "She doesn't know?"

"That I'm here?" Louis asked.

Moira interrupted. "They have our sister."

"Ay, that's not surprising," the man said again.

"You know her then?" Moira asked. "This—this woman who took my sister?"

The man nodded. "Better than anyone."

Moira and I exchanged a look. *Who is he?* I signed.

"Who are you?" Moira asked.

"Ailill mac Máta," he said, sighing. "Former king of Connacht."

"King?" Moira repeated. "God. Do you mean . . . Does that make you . . . ?"

The weak white mist around Ailill flickered. "The last husband of Medb."

an dream ultach

THE ULSTER PARTY

bríd

One afternoon, I awoke from a mid-afternoon nap to find Fenora hovering over me, a frown on her face. "My mother has called for me. Will you come?"

Yawning, I dragged myself out of bed, shaking my dreams away. Ever since Medb had told me about Dad's deal, how she had found us, my dreams had become more intense. They always portrayed Dad in some sort of anguish, whether it be guilt, fear, or confusion. *Eighteen and coming into powers none of you understand.* That was what Medb had said of me and my sisters, and it was completely true. We created things, curios, magical items we didn't even realize were our doing. And I dreamed things that came true. I felt the wind in my veins. And Ríona . . . it sometimes seemed as if she knew exactly what you were thinking without any words exchanged. And Moira?

Well, maybe Moira would turn out to be special too if she could

stop worrying for two feckin' seconds.

"Bríd?" Fenora called anxiously from the door. The other girls were crowding around her, preparing to go along, but Fenora sought me out especially.

I blinked. "Sorry, sorry," I said, reaching for the fur cape Fenora had lent me. Shivering, I wrapped it around the red wool dress Fenora had also lent me. "I'm coming."

Outside, the street was busy with people and animals, children running, dogs chasing each other. Residents moved in and out of small roundhouses, each topped with a cap of smoke. Some turned to look as we passed. But Fenora didn't see them. At least she seemed not to. She headed straight for Ráth Cruachan, her usual gaggle of girls trailing behind. I fell somewhere in between, desperate to soak up everything I could.

There were more people than usual mulling around the doorway at Ráth Cruachan, and they threw glances at Fenora as we made our way inside. Medb was lounging on the throne, as she often was, but she was dressed in a sharp red dress I'd never seen before. Today, no cloak covered the intricate weaving on the shoulders and at the waist, and she was wearing her sleek black crown. One of the Maines chattered in her ear, but Medb wore a look on her face that said she was most definitely not listening.

"Ah, Findabair, come," she said, interrupting her son. He pressed a hand to his mouth and backed away.

Fenora strode toward her, eyeing the throng of people in the room, which included all of her brothers. "You called for me?"

The girls dispersed to the side of the room, and I wondered if I was meant to go with them or Fenora. I decided to stay out of the spotlight and scurried after the girls as they gathered behind a group of grown men discussing something serious in low voices.

Medb's gaze followed me to my spot, but she didn't say anything. Her eyes went back to Fenora. "Join your brothers, please. We're expecting guests any moment."

If Fenora's frown could have deepened, it would have. "Guests?" she repeated. Her fair eyebrows scrunched together, creating a little knot of apprehension. I felt the urge to say something funny, to smooth the knot away.

"A party from Ulster is due to arrive at any moment," Medb said.

Fenora's spine snapped upright, but I couldn't see the look on her face as she turned and made her way to her brothers.

I was going to ask one of the girls who exactly from Ulster—or feckin' anywhere—would be coming here, of all places, not to mention *how*, but I didn't have the time.

A group of men and a few women stormed in, and all conversation in the room ceased. Everyone in Ráth Cruachan turned to stare. The newcomers moved confidently into the room, coming to a standstill some distance from the throne. They wore furs, and their skin was covered in blue-tinted tattoos. One man sported a braided design right across his forehead. They were almost exclusively big and burly, and freckled. And covered in dirt and dust.

"You are very welcome to Cruachan," Medb said, standing. She didn't shout, didn't even speak all that loudly. But her voice was strong, and when she spoke, everyone strained to listen.

One of the shorter Ulster men stepped forward. He was older and leaned on a tall walking stick carved in an intricate pattern. As I followed the pattern up the staff, I realized it wasn't a staff at all. On top perched a sharp gray point. It was a spear.

"And our business?" the old man asked.

Medb nodded at him. "It has been communicated. Please, rest this night. We shall talk business after we have broken bread together."

I looked around me, but nobody else seemed to know what this business was either. Some of the men who'd been gossiping earlier, though, they looked uneasy. And my housemates were silent, a very uncommon state for this group of girls.

The old man looked at Medb for a long time, and Medb simply looked back. Behind him, the other Ulster men murmured and shifted. Whatever business they had seemed awfully important to them.

It felt arrogant to even think it, but I couldn't help myself—did this have anything to do with me? My sisters? The Morrigan?

It couldn't. We'd never even been to any of the counties in Ulster, the northern province of Ireland. Though our dad had been, on various occasions, for his "work." Which was really all about our magic, after all, wasn't it?

Maybe Medb was going to trade us for something more powerful. Pass us off for the Morrigan, when she knew our powers weren't truly useful. Accidentally creating mildly magical kitchen items, levitating in my sleep, having tragic visions of the future at inopportune times . . . how could any of that be valuable in Medb's quest for power?

When Medb's gaze wavered from the visitors, it wasn't to locate me—she glanced at Fenora.

The old man finally nodded. "Aye, we can agree to that," he said.

"If you'll get us something to drink as well."

"*Miodh*," Medb said, gesturing to one of her sons. Several of the Maines stepped forward to usher the newcomers out of the hall. Medb stood till they were gone, watching their every movement. Most of the people left in the hall were watching her. When she gave no further commentary, only sitting back on the throne, one arm perched on an armrest, her chin in her hand, people began to file out or gather in groups to whisper.

Fenora came toward us girls, and I was eager to get outside and ask her what all this was about, when Medb said, "*A leanbh?*"

It was loud enough that everyone in the room turned. But it wasn't clear which *leanbh*—or *child*—she was calling to her. I'd never heard her speak to Fenora that way, but she was looking at her now.

In true Medb fashion, she waited for everybody in the room to still. Then her gaze slid to its target: a tall, pale white girl with curly brown hair. Her name was Úna, and she lived in our roundhouse.

Úna looked around at the others, as if afraid to believe she was indeed the *leanbh* Medb wanted to talk to. Someone gave her a gentle shove, and she stumbled forward.

"Y-Yes, *mo bhanríon?*" Úna asked, just loud enough for Medb to hear from where she stood.

"You will do Findabair's hair each morning and again each evening," Medb said, "for as long as our guests are here."

Fenora's body was absolutely rigid. Medb noticed. She wasn't even pretending to look at Úna.

"You will also lay out Findabair's clothing each morning and have something new prepared each evening. You will help her bathe before each evening meal." Medb spoke faster. "It will also be your duty to ensure Findabair carefully preserves both her hair and her clothes for the duration. Any lapse will be considered your error." Finally, Medb's eyes slid back to the poor dark-haired girl.

"Y-Yes, *mo bhanríon*," Úna stuttered.

Medb nodded once, and Úna scurried back to the comfort of our group.

Fenora headed for the door, and the rest of us girls moved as one toward her. We were nearly outside when Medb's voice rang out once more. "Badb?"

I froze. Everything in me willed me not to respond to that name. But resisting wasn't going to help me find any answers. About my powers. About who I really was. What other option did I have?

Slowly, I turned to face her.

Her chin held high, Medb descended the stairs from her throne. She wore leather slippers, which made my stomach clench. Something important was going on if Medb wasn't barefoot. She stopped in front of me and looked me up and down. "This life suits you, *a leanbh*."

My head still felt heavy from the fruit-flavored mead that had preceded my nap. I couldn't tell if she was teasing me. Or was there a threat in there somewhere?

"What did you think of our visitors from the north?" she asked.

I hesitated, unsure what her design was. Because Medb always had a reason when she addressed you in public.

"I . . . uh, well, I didn't know there were other . . . communities like yours."

Medb narrowed her eyes at me. "You thought we were the only

ones?" She laughed and took another step toward me, her slippers whispering on the ground. With thin fingers, she picked up a lock of my straight black hair. It was still messy from sleep. "*A leanbh*, there are tribes of old all over Ireland. The tribes of ancient magic, but also the formerly mortal, having lost mortality through nefarious means. In hiding, either in plain sight or by the will of the gods. The *aos sí*, gods of old like Lú, they linger, too, hidden away in their mounds or a breath away in the Otherworld."

Gods of old like Lú? Oh, Louis, who are you? What have you done to us?

She dropped my hair, and her hand slid down my cheek. "It is a dire crime against you that you haven't known this since the day you first drew breath." She shook her head and strode away. Over her shoulder, she gave me one last gem of advice: "It's time to right the wrongs of your past, Badb."

beiдh дamhsa ann
THERE WILL BE DANCING

b r í d

In the food hall the next day, a diminutive brown-skinned girl next to Fenora nodded shyly toward the entrance and giggled, smiling at me as though I were in on the joke. The hall was full of people coming and going as usual, but the newly arrived Ulster group stood uncertainly in the doorway of the hall. Fenora saw them, her cheeks blushed pink, and she returned to the salmon in front of her.

"Do they need help, like?" I asked.

The other girl giggled again, and Fenora cleared her throat. "They'll manage," she said in as even a voice as she could muster. "They'll have more than their fill to eat soon, anyway. It is expected my mother will decree we shall feast for three days and three nights to welcome them."

"Three days and three nights?" I repeated. "Jaysus. That's a bit much."

"I would tend to agree." Fenora sighed, shoving a hunk of bread

into her mouth.

The newcomers moved toward the fire at the center of the hall.

"What exactly does three days and nights of feasting entail?" I asked carefully, my eyes not quite able to leave one particular visitor's bare chest. Several of the men were bare to the waist, buff and confident. And no longer covered in the dust of the road. "General party things?"

"Something like that," Fenora muttered.

"Dancing," the girl who had first noticed the visitors piped up. "Dancing and music. Storytellers, and the freshest harvest. And so much food you could cry. And, if we're lucky . . ." She snickered and her eyes danced back to Fenora. "Maybe some matchmaking!"

"Hush," Fenora snapped, and there was no amusement in her face.

The girl dropped her head immediately, chastised by her princess.

I watched Fenora. Her gaze went to the strangers in the corner and a heavy apprehension weighed on her as she took in each visitor. I didn't understand her worry, and she didn't seem obliged to explain it.

"Cheer up," I said, nudging her playfully. "You've never been to a party with me. This could be fun."

She only forced a smile and blinked at her food. I should have realized then that she already knew just what types of activities her mother deemed fun.

THAT evening, Medb asked Fenora and me to watch her servants collect the honey from her hives. More honey than usual would be needed for the guests and this three-day feast. There would be the freshest fruits dipped in honey, and more beeswax candles would be needed for festivities after nightfall. And, of course, all the honey in the world couldn't supply the city with enough mead.

I sat on a boulder near the edge of the field as the sun fell nearer the horizon and the servants moved quietly among the bee skeps in their frightening outfits, their faces obscured by the straw masks. The sun setting over Ráth Cruachan was a stunning sight. But my gaze, which automatically lifted toward the sky, wasn't taking in the beauty.

Where the feck is he?

Thick, gray clouds floated slowly across the late sun. Finbar was nowhere to be seen.

"I know what you search the heavens for."

I gasped. Medb stood beside me, as if out of thin air. My heart beat fast.

"He's gone," Medb said. "He built a nest near Ráth Cruachan while you were still below, and my people found him charming. There was much chatter about him at meal times. But he hasn't been seen for days now. He's left."

For one startled moment, I thought we were talking about my father. I shook my head to clear it. No, it was Finbar. *He left.* People were doing that an awful lot lately, weren't they? First, my father. Now Finbar.

"He wouldn't do that," I murmured. And as much as I believed Finny wouldn't leave me . . . He hadn't been seen in days, not by me, not by anybody . . . Not since I'd been released from my cell. "I don't think."

Maybe Finbar had gone to find Ríona and Moira when he could no longer find me. I had asked him to do that in the first place. Maybe he would bring them here. Maybe . . .

Medb raised her brows. "You have more faith in others than is strictly wise."

For a split second, I was sure Medb had done something to him. Hurt him? Killed him? But she turned away in the next moment, her eyes back on the bees. "Well, that's quite enough melancholy for one afternoon. Wallowing doesn't suit, Badb. You will learn to be alone."

My heart turned to stone in my chest. I was alone, wasn't I? Entirely alone.

I picked up my mead and stood, taking a long swig. It ran over my tongue in a sweet wave. *Alone.* I'd feared it all my life. But maybe it had its merits.

IT TOOK a long while for the fire to burn low that night, but when it finally did, throwing the room in enough darkness that I could be certain of privacy, tears burned my eyes. Curled up in my bed, wrapped in the old furs of a long-forgotten animal, the smoke trailing toward the ceiling, I couldn't hold back the tears. The wind inside me spiraled in little pathetic eddies.

Until the eddies dissipated entirely.

Finbar was definitely gone.

I couldn't stomp down the betrayal that flared in my chest. I was angry that Finbar could leave me here, to a fate uncertain, so easily. Even though I'd told him to do just that. For his own safety. Was I that selfish that I wasn't truly concerned for his well-being, and now that he might finally have sought it, I resented him for it?

And maybe it wasn't just Finbar I was angry with. My dad's face swam before me. His horror-struck face as he'd watched Bunrowan burn in my dreams. *You left us. You brought us to this point.*

The tears took me by surprise. I'd thought I was stronger than that.

An image of Medb, slouched on her throne, came to my mind. She sat there, cold and emotionless, for so much of the day. Even when she was outside, in her garden with the bees and the flowers, the things she spoke so poetically about . . . there was nothing about her to make you think she felt anything but a persistent apathy.

Was it any wonder? Look where she lived, how she lived, in a city that had once been so mighty, now scraping together a way of life in a forgotten corner of Ireland, hidden away as the world moved on. Maybe there were only so many losses one could take, I thought. So many disappointments. Before the heart turns to stone.

I didn't have any dreams at all that night. And when I woke, my body was heavy on my bed. I didn't wake up flying.

scéal grá
LOVE STORY

moira

"Does it seem a little like he's . . . in hiding?" Ríona signed to me. Faolan gave a low growl, the red fur on his nape bristling.

I nodded and murmured, "God, yes."

"Hm?" Ailill asked, turning toward us from a hot plate rigged up on the floor beside the boat's helm. He was making us all tea, one cup at a time, in a sad-looking little kettle. Ríona already held a chipped mug in her hands, eyeing the dark tea inside.

"No milk, I'm afraid," Ailill had explained with a shrug at the boat. "No place to keep it."

Louis moved forward to grab the next cup of tea and handed it to me. "Thanks," I murmured.

"Now get to it, Ailill," Louis said. "Time is of the essence."

"What exactly do you want me to tell them?" Ailill said, stepping back to the hot plate. I wasn't quite sure, but I thought he'd turned to

hide flushed cheeks. I looked at Ríona to see if she had any reaction to him. All I saw was sympathy.

Louis took a deep breath and stood tall. *"Chuile rud."* *Everything.*

"Well, you already know who I am—"

Ríona nudged me, reminding me to get answers to the questions we both had. I interrupted Ailill. "But why are you here?" Here, in a rundown boat on the Liffey, quite far from his queen in the ancient city in County Roscommon.

"That'd be your fault, that would."

"And why is that, pray tell?" I asked.

"Being married to a queen isn't easy, you know," Ailill said, crossing his beefy arms. "Never was. But it was a living. Marrying Medb was the key to the kingship. Many men had it before me, but eventually, she chose me." He nodded, as if we were going to challenge that claim.

"Comhghairdeas," I muttered. *Congratulations.* "Still don't see how that's our fault."

"I'm getting there, so I am," Ailill muttered, turning back to the hot plate to fire up another cuppa. "I was chief bodyguard for the royal couple and still as yet inexperienced when she took me for her lover—"

"They don't need to know that part," Louis broke in, pressing a hand to his temple. Conry gave a big yawn and rolled over on the deck of the boat. Faolan eyed him warily before returning to his upright position beside Ríona, completely on guard.

"You said to tell them everything, you did," Ailill protested. "And that's what brought everything that happened after."

"Fine, fine," Louis said, holding his hands up defensively.

"As I was saying, her husband at the time, old Eochaid Dala, he took offense to the new arrangement. Medb had special fondness for spectacle, and she was known to encourage her suitors to fight to the death. The crown, of course, was the prize. The poor sods never knew how short their reign would be."

He looked sadly around the cabin, and I wondered exactly how short his reign had been.

"Single combat by spear was the challenge Eochaid set, and it was easy to take him. He died a brave man, and the crown was mine." Ailill shrugged, as if killing a man were an everyday occurrence, and handed a cup of tea to Aidan. "I'm afraid that's all the mugs now. I'm not used to entertaining here, am I?"

"I'm fine," Louis said. "Just get on with it."

Ailill cleared his throat. "Seven sons, I gave her. And a beautiful daughter. I was the only man to give her the children she so desperately wanted." He turned his great back to us, and the pause was heavy. "Cruachan is a dangerous place to spend one's life. Especially when married to the immortal Great Queen."

"Immortal?" I repeated, just as Ríona squeezed my arm and Faolan whined. Was this Queen Medb truly immortal? What on Earth were we up against?

"Of course, there are those who are born so," Ailill said, looking pointedly at Louis, "and those who do wicked things to get there." He looked at his hands and shook his head sadly. "The story of Cruachan is a story of both. A story of centuries. Like all else in the old world, the old ways and the ancient kingdoms of Ireland fell out of favor. Cruachan, like many strongholds of the *sidhe,* disappeared into the fog.

The city grew and flourished—or watched the young move out never to return—depending on the decade, depending on the century. Those who came did so from all over the world. The Irish dispersed to every corner of the Earth, but their children, grandchildren, and great-great grandchildren would eventually feel the call back and find us at Cruachan."

"But Medb always wanted more," Louis said with a small grin. He sounded like someone who had once—and maybe still did—worship the Great Queen.

"Yes, that is the way of the goddess, isn't it?" Ailill said darkly.

"I'm still not totally clear what this has to do with us," I said, hoping to hurry this story along. Every moment we were not at Cruachan was a moment Bríd's life might be in danger.

"Would you mind your patience, will you?" Ailill said. The mugs each of us held were going cold, but none of us were interested in tea at the moment. "Though many other *sidhe* cities like Cruachan survived the ages all over Ireland, none were as close to the Land of Youth as we were. It kept Medb strong while other strongholds disappeared. But even the Land of Youth couldn't give her back the power she'd once held over Connacht. Nothing could. At least, that was what we thought. Until news of you lot turned up."

Ríona grabbed my hand again, and I squeezed hers back.

Ailill turned to face us and spent a moment looking over each of us.

"It was always said the Morrigu could grant or take away sovereignty. We had never needed it before. But the longer time marched on, the smaller our reach became. When word came that the

Morrigu lived again . . . well, Medb became obsessed with finding the Morrigu and using her power to break Cruachan out of the fog to regain some power over Ireland. I thought this was absurd, but she was egged on by plenty. Not least of all, her favorite enemy, her oldest friend, her *ollam*."

Ailill glared in Louis's direction.

"Everyone makes mistakes," Louis said quietly. He had the grace to appear ashamed. Not ashamed enough to make me trust him, though.

"What's an *ollam*?" I asked.

Ailill's smile split slowly, wider and wider. "Has he not told ye who he is?" His gaze darted back and forth between Louis and the rest of us.

Louis simply held up the arm with the triskele on it.

"Well, well, well." Ailill laughed, a loud, shaking bark. "You lot are looking at Lú, god of sun and storms; the great Cú Chulainn; Louis, *ollam* of Cruachan.

Ríona squeezed my hand harder. I wasn't a fan of fairy tales, but you didn't need to be to know the name Cú Chulainn. He was one of Ireland's best known warrior heroes of myth. I looked to Ríona for guidance, to see if she was signing anything for me to pass on to the others, but she was just staring, her mouth wide open.

"Are you . . . are you trying to say Louis is Cú Chulainn?" I asked with a scoff. "*The* Cú Chulainn?" Ríona wouldn't loosen her grip on my hand.

Louis was grinning at us now, clearly proud to have finally gotten around the triskele.

"Do you know anything of the old Celtic ways?" Ailill asked.

"Even at Cruachan, the old gods are often mocked for their beliefs and practices. But I'm of the old guard, too, and one thing we hold to is the reincarnation of the gods. The gods don't live forever in the common sense, but their souls come back to us, life after life. It's long been held that Cú Chulainn was a reincarnation of his father, Lú. And Louis here is just the latest."

He gave a little shrug, like that followed the path of a logic so widely accepted that we couldn't possibly argue.

"Got it. You're telling us Louis is a god *and* the reincarnation of the legendary Cú Chulainn. Much easier to believe than an immortal queen." I looked at Ríona and threw my arms in the air.

She pressed her lips together, eyes wide, and looked at Louis. He'd already been watching her, his eyes shining. I felt like tearing my hair out. Or, at the very least, running to find Bó and getting out of here.

"Something tells me you don't believe the ways of old," Ailill said, crossing his arms. He lifted his chin to look at me down the length of his crooked nose. "You wouldn't be alone in that, but I'd challenge you to reconsider. After all, Louis's story isn't so very different from your own."

My heartbeat picked up, but too many questions entered my head at once to pin down just one. "What do you mean?"

"I mean that those who live to keep our histories alive, our bards, our *ollam* here, they say you are the reincarnation of the Morrigan. That is why Medb seeks you. That is why you find yourself in this place of danger. So you best start believing in your own destiny, *a leanbh*."

My heart was fluttering up near my throat. Reincarnation? Gods? This was too much. I didn't want to hear anymore. I just wanted Bríd back. Once we were together again, we could figure out exactly what these stories meant. We could find our father and get him to tell us our real history. How we had each ended up in the castle by the sea.

But first, you need to save Bríd.

Suddenly, I felt the full weight of what we intended to do: break into an ancient hidden city we'd never even seen before and rescue a prisoner.

Louis cleared his throat. "Ailill, don't go threatening them. Just tell them how you ended up here."

"Well, once Medb learned of you, I was redundant, so I was," Ailill explained. "Marriage is a powerful tool, and it was clear an empty crown up for grabs served her interests much better than I could. Luckily, I was used to living with Medb, and I heard the assassin's footsteps long before he found me in the dark of my bed."

Ríona's eyes were as round as Faolan's, shining in the moonlight.

"She tried to have you killed?" I asked.

"If she'd wanted me dead, I'd be dead," Ailill said. "She just wanted to give me a fright. Scare me off. And it was enough. Here I am, as you see me before you now."

Living alone on a boat slowly sinking into the Liffey.

I waited for Louis to say something, but he didn't. He just looked calmly across the deck at me and Ríona. He'd been right to bring us here. This man probably knew more about Medb than anyone. Except perhaps Louis himself. But he was no good to us while bound by some strange ancient oath magic.

Sighing deeply, I looked at Ríona. *"What do we do now?"* I signed to her.

She gave me a little shrug. *"We need him."*

I nodded once and turned back to Ailill. "Medb has our sister. We're going to rescue her. But we don't know what we're up against. You know Medb better than anyone. Will you come with us?"

Ailill twisted a strand of his beard between two fingers. "You're going to sneak into Cruachan and steal away a hostage of Medb's?"

I pursed my lips. "Well, yeah. We don't really have another option."

"I knew you lot were ill fated the moment you showed up." Ailill gave me a sad smile. "That'll have to be a *no* from me."

féasta do na déithe
A FEAST FOR THE GODS

bríd

The hall atop An Ráth Mór opened before me, but it was no longer an ordinary food hall. It was transformed. It was packed to the rafters with people, the air thick with smoke and a heady aroma I couldn't identify. Beeswax candles burned on every surface, and the long tables were pushed to the walls, leaving an open swath of floor. People danced, but others sat at the tables, so many people, and they weren't really sitting but lounging. On one, a woman laid full out as the people around her ate berries off her every limb. The next table over, a man stood on the tabletop between two skeins of wine, enticing his dog into dancing on its hind legs with a bit of turkey.

And behind everything—the music. Raucous songs came from a cluster of men on different instruments—a tin whistle, a fiddle, a huge harp, and a steady *bodhrán*—rollicking along and taking swigs of beer between notes.

For the first while, I followed Fenora around. The other girls were scattered throughout the crowd, apparently aware of their freedom for the night. And the boys of Cruachan seemed to be feeling freer as well. They stepped up to Fenora with uncharacteristic courage and spoke to her, or me, asking playful questions and teasing us about our answers.

I kept waiting for someone to call us to dinner, but after a while, it was clear the "three-day feast" was just that. People were eating constantly. There was fresh fruit and strange cheeses and warm bread, and honey, so much honey. Activity swirled around the roasting spits, and people walked around eating meat off the bone with their bare hands. I watched one young Ulsterman use a tiny dagger to swipe a juicy chunk off the meat his friend was holding.

After a while, the room hushed, and the music went quiet. An ornate carved chair had been placed at a long table on one side of the room. Several smaller chairs were occupied to either side, and as the crowd parted, I saw Medb stand behind the table.

"*Fáilte*," she said, her voice never rising to a yell. It didn't have to. Everyone in the room hung on her every word. "To our friends from the north, we bid you a fine stay."

I glanced at the Ulster group. They stood out, and they were certainly enjoying themselves. One man, bare to the waist, was fast asleep on the floor. His companions were busy burying him in the hay.

"We find ourselves, yet again, without our *ollam* tonight," Medb said, pursing her lips, and more than a few people in the crowd chuckled, scoffed, or whispered. "But all is not lost. Though the skill of our *ollam* be legendary, some might say it wanes. As old things do."

The whispers grew louder and there was outright laughter. It felt mean, though I didn't know whom they were talking about.

"Instead, tonight, we divert ourselves with these fine musicians and the bards and *fili* who will one day replace old Lú."

They were talking about Louis? He was this ollam *they spoke of?*

"Hear, hear!" somebody called.

"Yes," Medb said, smiling. "We hope our fine city entertains our visitors. And we shall address their concerns in due time." Medb raised a flagon from the table. "But first, let us see to full bellies and dizzy heads."

"*Sláinte!*" people across the room called out. Others cheered, and the crowd started moving again, a dizzying crush of bodies, as the *bodhrán* took up a beat once again.

I wanted to ask Fenora about Louis, about who he was and where they thought he'd gone. I knew the truth of where he'd ended up, of course. But did they know Louis had come to us? To Bunrowan? It didn't sound like they wanted him back. Did they know he'd turned traitor?

Of course they do. I remembered the first day I'd been here, when my kidnappers had dropped me at Medb's feet. They'd mentioned Louis. They'd told her how he'd helped us escape the siege on Bunrowan. How had I missed so much?

Unfortunately, that was when the real dancing began. Not just in the open space, but on the tables and in every nook and cranny to be found. I didn't have a moment to grab Fenora's attention and ask about Louis before the boys were in front of us.

The first boy to ask me for a dance was a tall, lithe figure with a head of carefully coiffed brown hair. Pursing my lips, I looked to

Fenora for some guidance on whether I should accept, but I found myself quite alone.

Fenora was nowhere to be seen. That was all right. I'd never met a boy who could faze me. None of these could be any worse than Brian Brennan back in Ballyconneely.

I pressed a hand to my own hairdo, a complicated braid set with tiny pearly stones. Fenora's pale white girl with the brown curls had sought the help of a friend to finish the complicated pattern, and to my surprise, the friend looked to be of East Asian descent. I remembered our mother's long treks to the nearest hair salon that could work with her hair, and how tired the three bus connections made her. That was why I'd been so surprised to see people who looked like her, and me, and people of all races, in Cruachan. How had they all ended up here?

"Well," I said, turning back to the boy. "Do you take longer than me to get ready for a party like this, d'you think?"

The boy only laughed and held out a hand. A sign of a good sense of humor. One point to ancient hill boys. "That's how it should be, should it not?" he said, laughter in his eyes and his dimples. "A lady as naturally beautiful as you shouldn't need to add anything to what the gods have given her. But a poor wretch like me?" He laughed again and dashed into the dance, pulling me along with him.

I didn't know any of the steps and nearly stumbled, for his feet were quick. But his hands were solid on my waist as he pulled me into each step.

The music was loud and the *bodhrán* vibrated in my bones. I felt drunk, I felt alive, I felt . . . powerful. For the first time in as long as I could remember, I felt like me.

Of course, I had been drinking quite a bit of mead. Nectar of the gods, indeed.

My dance partner's hand was scarcely off my waist when another replaced it. "That was beautiful, Cormac, but I'm afraid we're going to have to show the lady something a little livelier if she's going to be impressed with the entertainment at Cruachan."

I was spun into his arms before I could muster a witty retort, and I was delighted to see a handsome face before me.

"Hm, do I not get a say in it?" I asked, pretending to pull back.

Cormac laughed behind us. "She's the one in charge, Darragh."

My new dance partner, Darragh, pouted, dropping his hands. He was a tall Black boy with sharp cheekbones and a quick smile. "Should you sit a single dance out, it will prove us most unentertaining. In fact, I'm not sure our dear musicians here will ever forgive you. First we lose our legendary *ollam*, and now our reputation as well?"

I pursed my lips, as if thinking, and then extended my hand. "I suppose, when you put it that way . . ."

"It's true," he said, a hand on his heart. "Besides, if you don't dance, how else will they write poems about you?"

Laughter spilled out of my throat as my new dance partner dipped me back to the point of nearly tripping and just as quickly rushed me into the mesh of bodies stepping in time with the musicians.

Had it always felt this good to dance? To parade a handsome boy around a room full of eager eyes?

I couldn't remember. I couldn't remember much of anything at the moment. For my next suitor was lining up.

As he extended his hand and offered me a wink, I looked behind him, my eye catching Medb's. She was smiling—actually, fully smiling. I was turning to the next boy in line when Medb herself materialized before me. She held her drink in front of her and tilted her head to gaze at me.

"You feel it, don't you?"

I stared at her, my cheeks warm.

"Intoxicating." She took a swig from her cup and shook her head. "That's what they called me. Because they couldn't resist me. I brought a joy and a power and a life they couldn't fathom. And also sometimes destruction." She shrugged, like that was the price one had to pay sometimes.

The bare-chested man from the Ulster Party was behind Medb, whispering something in her ear.

Medb licked her lips and grinned at me, a little sardonic smile like we had an inside joke. Then she turned and gave her hand to the Ulster man, who began to pull her away. She paused in the crush of the crowd and turned back to me. "You are Badb," she said. "I know you feel it too."

I felt breathy and high, like I was soaring through the sky, as high as Finbar, and would never come down. Medb disappeared in the crowd.

"A dance?" someone asked over my shoulder.

I didn't play coy this time. This boy looked suspiciously like a Maine, but I didn't care. I grabbed his hand and dragged him into the dance.

When his hands had grown so sweaty he could barely keep hold of me, I paused to catch my breath. "I think you've had your share, lad," I said.

"Aye," he agreed. "And you've got your next partner awaiting my departure."

Someone passed a mug of beer to him over my shoulder, and he took it gratefully as the next dancer slid two hands around my waist and twirled me into the crush of bodies that had already begun the next dance.

Eyes closed, I spun and spun and felt I'd never stop. And I didn't want to. This was beyond any awkward kiss with Brian Brennan at a town festival. This was different.

My partner steadied me with firm hands on my waist, and I opened my eyes to look into the red-tinted face of Fenora.

The breath caught in my throat. Her hair was down, and the blonde strands along her face were dark with sweat. Little beads of ivory sat in her hair like drops of rain. "I'm not sure I know this one," I said breathlessly.

Her head tipped back the tiniest bit as she laughed. "I've been watching you," she said, and my heart flipped over. "You don't know any of them."

I scoffed in surprise and swatted at her shoulder. "Are you saying I can't dance?"

"I'm saying you're the most prolific dance partner on the floor tonight," she said with a sweet smile. "That is all."

As we talked, I didn't fail to realize that Fenora kept us moving in sync with the others, never missing a step. Where had she learned to dance like this?

"Well, maybe if I'd had better partners, I would be getting the hang of it a little quicker."

"Better partners?" Fenora repeated. "You've danced with every one of Cruachan's finest tonight."

"Really?" I grinned. "Have I danced with fine young men and not even known it?"

Fenora laughed. "Your first," she said, "is considered one of the top picks currently available to the daughter of Medb."

My eyebrows shot up. "Really? He was a slippery one, I'll say. I don't think he suits you."

"No?" Fenora asked.

I shook my head. "Not your match."

Fenora shook her head, her cheeks pink. "No, I don't believe he is."

The eddies in my veins picked up, and this time, it didn't feel as though I would fly away from here, but rather that we would dance right into the air, Fenora's hand in mine.

suiríocha ríoga
ROYAL SUITORS

bríd

We were the last ones awake, Fenora and I. The rest of the house on Ráth da Dtarbh was quiet and dark, and tiny shadows danced on the walls from the flames left in the fire. We'd left An Ráth Mór to those more inebriated than us and skipped home beneath the stars. Most of the girls had fallen asleep right away, but I lay on my cot watching the smoke dance toward the ceiling and escape out into the night. Through the hole in the ceiling, I could see a few stars winking down at me.

Sometimes I wished I could jump into the air and join them. Other times I wondered if Finbar was out there, looking back at me, hidden just out of sight. But mostly, I thought about the feeling of dancing around An Ráth Mór in the arms of a stranger. Or Fenora.

She sat beside me combing out her hair with an intricately carved comb. It looked suspiciously like it had been carved from bone.

"You told me once that you were lonely," I said, thinking of the

stars all the way out there, all alone. And me and my sisters at Bunrowan, tucked away under many more stars than that. "How could you be?" I asked, nodding at the sleeping figures around us. "With all of them?"

Fenora sniffed. "One can be alone in a sea of people," she said softly, working through a knot at the end of a long, thin braid in her otherwise loose hair. "Besides, sometimes it is precisely when I'm surrounded by people that I feel most alone."

I remembered how she'd looked, that characteristic frown of hers in place, when we'd been bombarded with curious boys and dance partners earlier this evening. "You don't like the attention?" I asked. "I've always rather enjoyed it."

Fenora looked at me. "Do you ever tire of being seen through the eyes of frightened men?"

I blinked at her.

"That's what they are," she said. "Frightened. Scared that I have more power than them. That I have the power to determine their fate. Don't you feel that?"

Of course I did. I'd always been beautiful, and boys had started paying me attention much too young. Which was why I'd felt compelled to wield it. And it had become my power. If you didn't tease them, dance with them on your terms, stare right back, tease right back, you had no power. At least, that was what I'd always thought.

Before I could gather my thoughts to respond, Fenora sighed and dropped her comb. "My future is signed away," she said.

I sat up. "What do you mean?"

"I've been betrothed to a lad called Liam since I was little. He's the son of an old god in Ulster."

"An old . . . god?" I repeated.

"You've a lot to get used to here," Fenora said softly.

"That's an understatement. Is he . . . here?" I asked, wondering about each man I'd danced with tonight. Had one of them been Fenora's future husband?

But Fenora shook her head. "Not that I know of."

"Not that you know of?" I repeated. "Do you mean . . . you don't know what he looks like? You've never met him before?"

"No, and I hope not to until it cannot be helped. At least then I can pretend for a little longer that my life is my own."

"Is this a secret?" I asked. "Men are always vying for your attention. I've noticed it even in the short time I've been here. Do they not know?"

"Ambition never dies," Fenora said, propping her chin on her fist. "It's no secret. But it's also no secret that my mother respects marriage the way a dog respects cats."

I almost asked about her father again, but my mind was running in too many directions at once. "Betrothed," I breathed. "Jaysus."

Her face was bent over her hands in her lap, where she fiddled with her comb.

I reached a hand out and stilled her fingers. One of the girls rolled over in her sleep, and Fenora jumped. We watched the girl settle again in the dying light of the fire.

"Your life is still your own, Fenora," I whispered.

She smiled weakly. It wasn't a whole smile, just a gentle loosening of her frown.

"We should sleep," Fenora said, standing up. She turned to make her way to her own cot, but first, she bent and kissed me on the cheek. "Good night, Bríd."

The spot on my cheek burned as I lay down on my cot and desperately thought the words over and over again: *Your life is still your own. Your life is still your own.*

I just hoped it was true. For Fenora and for me.

IT TURNS out the debauchery doesn't stop for a moment during a three-day feast. When our group of girls made it to An Ráth Mór for breakfast, there were drunk courtiers happily curled up under tables and around the fire, completely asleep. Apparently, falling asleep wherever you may be when you become tired was considered a logical thing to do. Some of the other girls took up last night's activities once again as soon as we'd eaten, but Fenora and I begged off for rest and spent a quiet day in the roundhouse.

We also took a walk along the main thoroughfare of Cruachan, which led past so many small roundhouses that I began to wonder just how many people lived here. We talked of many things, but mostly Fenora. Her life here, the things she wished for and dreamed of. Like traveling outside Cruachan and starting a garden and raising her own animals and living a life outside of strangers' notice. I had a tendency to promise her all those things were possible, without really believing it myself. Who was I to tell someone what was possible? I'd never seen the world outside Bunrowan until now.

By the time we returned to An Ráth Mór in search of food, the party was in full tilt yet again. And it felt like there were more people in attendance than last night, if that were possible.

Medb was presiding at the long table. She sat, looking bored, her attention wandering, as people stepped to a spot in front of her and spoke, probably begging for this or that. I thought about moving closer to eavesdrop, but just then, Medb caught me staring. She wasn't smiling, exactly, but she nodded at me. I had the feeling that my behavior was pleasing her.

I didn't know if that was a good or bad thing.

"M'lady!" A boy jumped in front of me and Fenora, all bright, eager eyes. "You're back," he said. His eyes were bright, to be sure, but also swimming with drink. And he was smiling at Fenora like an eejit.

"Is your name Liam?" I asked him.

Fenora let out a burst of laughter, and then looked surprised at herself. True enough, a laugh from Fenora had to be earned. She shook her head. "This is no Ulsterman. This is a Cruachan lad," she told me.

"Aye," he said, a bit confused, "and it should be none other who wins your first dance tonight."

A pale, long-fingered hand came down on the boy's shoulder, and he looked delighted. Until he turned and found that his would-be surprise dance partner was Queen Medb herself. He hastily bowed and mumbled a nonsensical excuse, stumbling away before I could tease him.

"Well, Findabair, you have decided to join us after all," Medb said.

"You made it quite clear it was expected of me," Fenora replied.

"And you took that to mean you could make short, flippant appearances whenever it suited you?" Medb shook her head. "Your future lies in this room, Findabair."

"I won't marry Liam. I won't do it!" The declaration came out like a splinter, a shred of dignity wedged beneath Fenora's skin for so long she'd forgotten she could let it loose.

My heart sped up, and the wind in my veins swirled, a desperate, scared thing, ready to lift the both of us off our feet and fly out the hole in the ceiling if it came to that.

But Medb only laughed. "Oh, my dear Findabair." She shook her head. "It's a pretty declaration that matters not."

Medb turned and walked away. The empty spot she left behind was swallowed by the crowd. I glanced at Fenora. Her cheeks were red from her outburst, but her mouth was open in surprise. Before she could collect herself, the boy was back, asking for a dance or two or three.

"Please," Fenora said, turning away from him. "I just want peace."

The music fell away to a steady drumbeat that interrupted the raucous revelry, including whatever plans this boy had had for Fenora's evening. As silence fell, the drumbeat petered out, and all eyes in the room found Medb, who stood before her chair, the same half-smile on her lips.

"*Fáilte*," Medb said, her voice loud, firm, even. Always even. Did the woman ever experience emotions? "I trust you all have been enjoying yourselves," she went on, her roving gaze landing on a knot of the Ulster visitors who were clashing spears in a rousing bout of play. At least I hoped it was play. "I'll interrupt the festivities for only a moment. I wish to present a challenge."

All around us people began to stir, a low hum starting up. Beside me Fenora made a strangled sound. Her face was pale.

"What is it?" I whispered uneasily.

She shook her head. "My mother has a bit of a reputation for her challenges."

A group of Fenora's brothers lingered nearby. Case in point. All seven of them had been renamed for the sole purpose of Queen Medb's attempt to challenge fate. To fulfill the prophecy of a man's death. What wouldn't this woman do?

Medb let the excitement build for a moment. She waited for the whispering to die down, and people began to shush each other. She was always in control of every single moment. It would have been impressive if it weren't so terrifying.

"I'm sure you all remember our dear *ollam*, who won't be returning to fair Cruachan," Medb said.

A sound of disappointment rippled through the crowd, but it was too loud, too theatrical. They were mocking Louis.

"Yes," Medb said. "It's a tragedy indeed. But you all know traitors cannot be suffered in Cruachan. For that reason, I lay this challenge before you: the first man to best our fair *ollam*, our dastardly Cú Chulainn, in combat will have my beautiful daughter's hand in marriage."

Excited chatter broke out. Nobody bothered to whisper. Medb gleefully turned away, to let the excitement transform into other, more raucous merrymaking activities. But my eyes were on Fenora.

Her face was slack, her mouth open in her gentle pout. It wasn't so much surprise on her face as anguish. As if she would have expected nothing less from her mother and Medb had finally delivered.

"Fen—"

Before I could stop her, she was dashing across the room toward her mother. But Medb was moving for the door, oblivious to the raging princess bearing down on her. The crowd slowed Fenora's progress, and she shoved people out of the way to reach her mother.

I was only a step behind her, but by the time I reached the door, Medb was gone, and Fenora was flying down the stairs.

FENORA burst through the doors into Medb's apartments. "How could you?" she shrieked.

I was two steps behind her.

Eyebrows raised imperiously, Medb looked up from the conversation she'd been having with a man who sat on the floor beside her chair. "Well, Findabair, I'm not sure who taught you to enter a room like that, but it most certainly was not your queen mother."

"You have lost your wits. Finally, you have truly lost whatever was once inside your head. I won't do it!"

"You won't do this, you won't do that," Medb said, tipping her head one way and then the other. "Why is it that all I hear from you today is what you *won't* do? Tell me, Findabair, what *will* you do?"

Fenora faltered, her anger propelling her forward, but she didn't know which direction to take. "I . . ." She glanced at me. "I'll leave Cruachan and start a garden and buy my own animals and never step foot here again."

Medb stared at her for a moment. Then she shrieked in laughter.

I recoiled, the sound so alien and unexpected, I was sure it hadn't come from Medb at all.

"That . . ." She continued to laugh. "That was very diverting.

Thank you ever so much."

"You can't make me," Fenora cried, bending at the waist, her arms wrapped around herself like a desperate child. Her anger had transformed to desperation so quickly, I didn't know what to do. What she needed.

"Oh?" Medb stood and was towering above her daughter in a mere second. Fenora cowered. "Do you really believe that to be true, *my dearest* Findabair? That I can't *make* you do it?"

All pretense of laughter was gone, and Medb looked downright terrifying. Her eyes flashed, her mouth a thin slit spitting venom. And I believed her. I couldn't imagine Fenora besting this raging queen at anything.

"But the truth is I won't have to *make* you," Medb said.

Fenora curled in on herself even more, her shoulders heaving. Medb barely moved, an inhuman stillness about her.

"We both know you will do what I say when the time comes. And that is as it should be. Until then, cry and rail as you like. Dream of pigs and vegetables or whatever it is you want—even Liam, if that seems a fairer option now. I do not care. Gods know it doesn't matter to me how you spend the last days of your freedom. Because that's what it will be, Findabair. Days. The time of Ailill, the time of Conchobar, the time of Louis, is over. And you will spend your life with the victor. Cruachan deserves no less."

She didn't give her daughter—or me—another look. Merely spun on the spot, her skirts twirling, and marched back to her spot and her companion.

Fenora didn't move, except for the sobs that wracked her body. I slid an arm around her middle and guided her toward the door. "*Oya,*" I whispered. "Come on, let's get out of here."

Fenora straightened and looked me in the eye. She licked her cracked lips and stopped crying.

"What? What is it?" I asked. We were just barely out of earshot of her mother.

"Let's get out of here," Fenora whispered.

I only stared at her. That's exactly what I was trying to do. Why was she stopping? The warmth of the roundhouse on Ráth da Dtarbh would be comforting to us both tonight.

"Out of here," Fenora repeated. "Out of Cruachan."

sinsir

ANCESTORS

ríona

"I can't believe he said *no*," Moira muttered, crossing her arms over her chest and kicking at the wood panel along the edge of the boat. Her disappointment felt sharp. "Some king he is." Dark blue clouds swirled around her arms and legs. She was itching to do something—something to save Bríd, but she knew whatever lay ahead was terrifying.

I glanced back at the cabin. Louis was gesticulating wildly, trying to convince Ailill to come with us. But every so often, Louis fell silent and his arms dropped to his sides, as if he'd run into another wall with the triskele.

A pale mist circulated around Ailill, a tired fog that infected my own body and made everything feel slower. It seemed as though Ailill had given up on life. That probably meant he was immune to Louis's wheedling.

Aidan caught my eye. He stood awkwardly outside the door of the

cabin, opposite Conry, who yawned and sat down. The two of them looked like a pair of untrustworthy sentries. My heart fell. There was no way we could charge into Cruachan alone.

I turned back to Moira. *"We just need to convince him,"* I signed. *"Maybe play to his emotions as a father."*

Moira rolled her eyes. "He was married to Medb for centuries," she cried. "Do you really think he has an altruistic bone in his immortal body?" Her nose scrunched up as she said it, as if being immortal were the same as being a zombie.

"What about Louis's 'powers of persuasion'?" I signed.

Moira pressed her lips together. "If he were going to help, he'd have done it by now."

Faolan whimpered, and a shiver ran up my spine. I shook my head out like Faolan did when people touched his ears. Thinking about everything Ailill had told us, about himself, about us, about Louis, was the last thing I wanted to do right now. It was hurting my brain. We needed to concentrate on the danger of the here and now—which needed to include saving Bríd.

"Moira, do you find it weird . . ." I paused, scared to form the rest of my thought.

"That we haven't seen Finbar?" Moira whispered.

Faolan whimpered again, and I buried my hand in his fur. *"Why hasn't she sent him to us?"* I asked.

"Maybe she has," Moira said, biting her lip. "Maybe he couldn't track us."

I let that be the last thought, even though neither of us believed it. Finbar could find any of us. Once, when we'd been much younger,

Moira had been angry over something Bríd had said or done and gone tramping off alone. We hadn't thought to worry until the sun had gone down. A normal family may have called the police. But at Bunrowan . . . Dad had asked Finbar to find her, and she'd shown up at the door with Finbar on her shoulder not thirty minutes later.

If Finbar hadn't come to find us, something was wrong. We had to do something.

With a decisive nod, I signed to Moira, *"We need to go to the pub."*

Exasperated, she held her arms wide. "Your big plan is to get Bríd's rescuers drunk? *Abeg,* how would that help?"

"Ailill is sad and lonely," I signed. *"He'll eventually agree to a job that will take him back home, even if it's dangerous. As long as he doesn't get tripped up by reason. Reason won't get in the way if he's drinking."*

Moira sucked on her bottom lip. I knew that meant the idea wasn't half as stupid as she'd first thought it to be. "You think he'll agree to come?"

I nudged an empty beer can rolling back and forth on the deck every few minutes when the boat groaned and shifted in the river. *"It has to beat drinking alone."*

"I MAY spend more time than is wise in here," Ailill admitted, taking a deep gulp of his Guinness. The pub down the street from his boat was no more than a small storefront covered in peeling maroon paint from the outside, but once we stepped inside, a warren of booths and cozy tables was revealed.

Ailill had led us straight to a table near the back. He was clearly familiar with the place. Faolan had been perturbed to be left back at the boat with Bó, and I was antsy without him. Conry had been allowed to come along, since he didn't look so much like a wild wolf, and Louis had left him lazing in a patch of bluebells beside the front door to the pub.

As we sat, various people around the quiet bar had glanced at us, but only with passing interest. In Dublin, they were used to strangers often enough, even tourists and people from all over the world. Not like back in Connemara. The other patrons had all returned to their own conversations, each nursing a drink and a wobbly, watery aura of fatigue and general disappointment. The energy here was lax enough that I could tune out the feelings of the Dubliners with just a little effort. I wasn't the only one who gave a sigh of relief—Louis had seemed to let down his guard a bit too.

Ailill moved off to the bar and threw a request for an extra pair of hands over his shoulder. Moira narrowed her eyes at him, her suspicion jumping off her like sparks of fire. "I'll join you," she said. She squeezed my arm before stepping away from the table.

Aidan was right behind her. "Me too."

That left Louis and me sitting across the table from one another, awkwardly avoiding eye contact. A fire burned in an ancient hearth behind us. It was cozy and warm, and I couldn't help but think of the last time I'd felt this alone with Louis. Up on the parapets of the castle, when he'd first made me see myself as the golden girl in a castle by the sea.

"How are you feeling after hearing all of that?" Louis asked. His eyes were clear, his face open. It was still infuriating to me that I couldn't read him the way I could other people. I wondered if it was because of what Ailill had told us, about who Louis was—an Irish legend.

I pulled my notepad from my pocket and scribbled down, *Why won't you use your confoundment spell on Ailill? You used it on us.*

Louis smiled as he read, but it was a complex smile. It looked like it pained him. "Remember my sword? I haven't been able to summon it since we left Bunrowan. I feel . . . well, I feel weak." His eyes met mine very briefly. "It's true, what they say to taunt me. The ways of old are dying. My powers are dying."

My heart thundering, I wrote: *So you're really a god?*

Louis's sad smile was back. "It's not like in the modern sense," he said at last, scratching at the wooden surface of the table with a fingernail. "The Tuatha de Danaan . . ." He held his arm out and glanced down at the triskele.

We both waited. Nothing happened.

"The Tuatha de Danaan were a magical people who inhabited Ireland long ago." He waited again, timidly testing the bounds of the triskele, like sticking one foot in the sea before plunging headlong into the waves. "Like Ailill said, time and shifting power left them diminished and abandoned. They went underground, into the *sidhe*, the fairy mounds, and were reincarnated through the generations. Some of them moved out into the world and had children among the mortals. They came back, or they didn't. Sometimes their children did."

He looked down at the pad again, as if hoping I would say something. But I didn't know what to say. I sucked on my lips and finally wrote, *And you really believe my sisters and I are part of this other world?*

"You—" He gasped and clutched his arm.

Between his fingers, the triskele glowed bright red. Through clenched teeth, Louis sucked in a breath. The muscles in his neck stood out in his effort not to scream.

I scooted closer and grabbed his hand, which was hot to the touch. Just like I had when this had happened back in Bunrowan, I rubbed one thumb over the back of his hand. With my other hand, I rubbed his back. There was a commotion at the front of the pub, and in seconds, Conry was under our table, his head on Louis's knee. He whined low in his throat, and each breath of Louis's came a little easier.

"Hey! You can't let that dog in here." The barman slapped a towel over his shoulder and came marching our way. "Do you hear me?"

Louis was nearly breathing normally again, though he was hunched around his hand like a wounded animal. I waved a hand at the barman, and Conry gave a low grumble and headed for the door.

Ailill had returned, his hands full of overflowing pints. "What's wrong with you, lad?" He clunked the glasses down on the tabletop, spilling sticky beer across it. "Go on, Tom, the beast is going," he muttered at the barman.

Louis grimaced and met my gaze. "Tried to talk a little too much."

Fallen god, legendary warrior, whatever this boy was, there were depths to him that I wanted to uncover, triskele or not.

aimsiú nach bhfuilltear á iarraidh

AN UNWELCOME DISCOVERY

bríd

The rest of the girls were still feasting with the Ulster party. No doubt the merriment had only grown in timbre and excitement after the challenge had been presented. As Fenora had explained to me, winning the ultimate prize in such a pursuit was a surefire way to gain fame and glory. I only wished Fenora herself weren't that prize.

Though, to her credit, she no longer looked defeated. She clearly had a plan.

The roundhouse was empty, but I kept glancing carefully around, expecting to find someone listening.

"Are you sure you can do that?" I asked. Me escaping Cruachan was one thing. I would be going back to my sisters. But Fenora? She would be leaving behind everything she'd ever known.

"I'm sure," she said, and her blue eyes had never looked so bright.

"But . . . but how?" I asked. It wasn't like Fenora's mother had security on the roundhouse at all times—that I knew of—but still, Fenora wasn't exactly a person who could pass through Cruachan undetected. Feck, I didn't even know how I'd gotten here. Much less how to get out.

My head spun with all the details I'd never contemplated. All I had wanted since the moment I'd found myself here was to get away. But I'd never considered the particulars. I'd always just assumed my sisters would find me. In fact, I hadn't tried to make my own escape at all. Did that mean . . . maybe my will to leave wasn't all that strong after all?

"It will be easy," Fenora said excitedly. "Tomorrow, the last day of the feast, will be the rowdiest. They'll get so drunk they won't be able to even think about business until the following day. And while they're making merry, we'll simply walk out. Nobody will be paying attention, least of all my mother, who is no doubt at this very moment trying to ascertain how best to swindle the Ulster guests."

Nerves twisted in my stomach, but there was something else too. Excitement. Walking out of here with the queen's daughter was foolishness.

But it just might work.

"And you know . . . how to?" I asked. "How to get from here to . . . to where I'm from? My . . . time?"

"I've told you before, ya dope, you haven't traveled through time." Fenora smiled. Her gentle teasing made my cheeks feel warm. "The veil between our worlds is thin. I've never crossed it myself, but I know how."

"Does it involve any . . . sacrifice?" I asked, scrunching my nose.

Fenora laughed, and her rare laughter was like an angel ringing a tinkling bell. "Of course not. Just the right words and a bit of a shove."

"I remember the shove," I grumbled.

Fenora took my hand. "Will you do it? Will you go with me?"

"Of course," I said, my heart warming to the plan. "We'll find my sisters and decide what to do next. We'll have to go somewhere your mother won't find you." Where she wouldn't find any of us.

"Yes," Fenora said, squeezing my hand. "We'll find somewhere safe. Together."

I MUST have fallen asleep as soon as my head hit my pallet, happiness thrumming through me along with the wind in my veins. It was the dream that woke me.

I wasn't flying. I was walking, two feet on the ground. On a smooth mud floor, to be exact. And then I was staring through the bars of a small iron cage. It was no bigger than a hatbox, and something small hopped around inside.

Strange, I thought. To keep something so small and harmless locked up.

I moved closer, trying to see through the bars in the dark. The room didn't look familiar. There was a chair in one corner, but the walls were barely wide enough to fit me and the chair. It was more of a closet, really. And if I was very quiet—held my breath—I could hear a low hum. The bees. I must have been in Medb's hall on Ráth Cruachan.

I caught a whiff of food—vegetables, and the heavy tang of meat. Near the kitchens? My eyes were adjusting to the dark, and when I crouched in front of the cage, shiny black eyes stared out at me.

A small voice squeaked, "*Abeg?*"

Something inside me snapped in two.

And then I was standing barefoot in our room on Ráth da Dtarbh. All was dark. I couldn't remember falling asleep or waking up from the dream, but time had passed around me. The girls were asleep, the fire was out, and there was a tornado within me.

I didn't stop to think, to feel, to question. I just ran. I ran along the quiet streets, past singing drunk people, a few dogs, and a handful of scattered chickens, to Ráth Cruachan.

At the bottom of the steps, I paused. Two men stood outside the closed door, swords at their hips. Of course Medb's home would be guarded at night. Biting my lip, I backed up a few paces before making a split-second decision.

Instead of charging blindly into Medb's private quarters like an eejit, I would go to the kitchens. Circling to the back of the mound, I climbed over the wooden fence at the foot of the hill and made my way up the slope. It was steep and studded with rocks, which made me fall several times. But the moonlight led me easily to the back field where the bees were kept. I sprinted down the rocky path to the kitchen door.

There was no guard here, but there would probably be one inside, nearer where Medb slept. Lacking any better plan, I peeked inside to see what I was dealing with. Two kitchen maids were scrubbing away at something in a bucket, but they seemed only half-awake and quite put out to be working the night shift.

And I'd seen them before. Which meant they'd probably seen me. They knew who I was. That I was close with Fenora. Was that a good thing or a bad thing?

I decided there was only one way to find out.

"Oh, hiya," I said, stepping inside.

Both girls looked up in fright. When they saw me, they seemed to relax. "What can we get you?" one asked as they both went back to the task at hand.

They thought I was there for a midnight snack. "I, uh, I was trying to sleep but couldn't quite get past the rumbling in my stomach. Do you have anything I could munch on?"

"*An cairéad*, to be sure," one said, climbing to her feet and going to find the carrots.

I looked frantically around. There were three doors off this room, and I already knew where one led. Edging toward the second, I watched the kitchen maids' movements. The first was moving toward the second door—a pantry?—and the other had slumped back over her task in the bucket, too tired to pay me any mind.

Without a better plan, I decided I had to go for it—I opened the last door. "*Abeg*, please be here," I whispered.

"What are you doing?" the girl at the bucket asked, warily climbing to her feet. "We aren't supposed to go in there."

First, I saw that the room was really a small closet. Then I saw a chair. And the cage.

"*Abeg!*" Finbar squawked.

Something made of glass exploded behind me and the chair flipped over, as if by an immense wind. It felt like there was a tornado in my gut, and it was about to tear out of me and destroy everything in my sight. Tears streaming down my face, I grabbed the cage and ran.

an dara impíoch
THE SECOND SUPPLICANT

ríona

"Have you heard this lad speak?" Ailill asked, brandishing his pint-bearing arm toward Louis and spilling half of it in the process. He was getting progressively chattier, which played directly into our plan. But that was about as far as the plan went. "I mean *really* speak. He can captivate a room, so he can. The best *ollam* Cruachan's ever seen, in my humble opinion."

Louis grinned, and his cheeks went a little pink. Just enough to look modest. I thought of the poem he'd given me at Bunrowan, and my stomach did a little two-step. It had caused quite enough drama in our household. Suddenly, I was glad Bríd wasn't here. Immediately, I felt guilty for even thinking it. What if she was in danger?

"You never explained what an *ollam* is," Moira said. She had a pint of something amber in front of her, but she was barely touching it. I'd forgone a pint completely and instead sipped at a glass of ice-cold

water.

"There's little a Celt loves more than a good story," Ailill said, slugging down half his remaining drink. "And this lad here was the greatest *fili* of them all. That's the name for our prophetic poets, that is. Our most elite bards and poets. The keepers of our history. Everything that happened to us, it was immortalized by the bards, the poets, the historians. And the *ollam* is the top of them all."

"Each chief chooses their own *ollam*," Louis explained. "To preside over the others."

"And the best of them all?" Ailill chuckled. "Ollamh Érenn. A gold bell-branch held above his head. With rights to dress as fine as the king."

Louis shook his head and chuckled, embarrassed.

"I remember the day we conferred the robe upon you, lad," Ailill said, taking another swig of beer. He put his pint down with a clunk and slapped a great palm on Louis's shoulder. He looked like a proud father ruminating on happier times. "It had to be him. He was a smith, a champion, a swordsman, a harpist, a hero, a poet, a sorcerer, a craftsman. Did I get them all?"

Louis gave him a sad smile in return. "I think so."

"How far we've come from that," Ailill said, nodding gently.

"It is better this way," Louis said. "You and I weren't made for a life like that. Ruthless. Cutthroat."

"Were we not?" Ailill heaved a great huffing laugh. "I seem to remember the both of us thriving a fair bit." His eyes had gone unfocused, like he was looking at something very far away—or very long ago. "But you're right—the past is not worth reliving. Not at this stage anyway."

That was a bit ironic, given that these men were, to us, literal figures from history. The past come alive.

"But you can't tell that to some people." Ailill shook his head. "You lot will be going up against a fierce force. The people of Cruachan, they're no army. But they are the modern *sidhe.*"

"What does that mean?" Moira asked. I looked at Louis, wondering if he would repeat what he'd told me, but his eyes were on the triskele.

"The *sidhe*, the faerie people of the mounds. Many in Cruachan are descended from the *sidhe* who left long ago and procreated with humans. Their descendants have returned at various points throughout the centuries. Even those who aren't magical are still loyal to the magic and the queen of old. They want Medb restored to power. They know our history through the songs and poems of the bards. That is a testament to the power of the *ollam.*"

"Do they know about us?" Moira asked.

Ailill shrugged. "I would think not. Medb keeps her plans close to her chest. They probably don't know that she believes the Morrigan is key to restoring her power."

"And what power is that exactly?" Moira asked.

Ailill exchanged a look with Louis, and their hesitance would have been clear even if I couldn't feel the fear emanating from them both. "It hasn't been seen in centuries. Nobody knows the truth of what a modern Ireland in the hands of Queen Medb would be. But it's a power that transcends Cruachan, you can be sure of that."

A shiver ran down my spine, and I instinctively put a hand out for the therapeutic touch of Faolan's fur. Of course, he wasn't there. I curled my fingers into my cold palm just as Aidan slammed his fist on the table. "We have to stop her!"

Moira looked at him like he was obtuse. Annoyance flickered off her. "We have to save *Bríd*," she corrected him. "That's what we have to do."

For a second, I thought I was about to witness Moira and Aidan's first argument. But then a feeling of foreboding came over me. I was blocking out as much emotion in the pub as I could, focusing on our table alone, but a sharp, giddy feeling was making its way through the bar. It was frantic and eager—too eager.

I grabbed Moira's arm. She turned to me, but the minute she saw the look on my face, her eyes darted around the pub. "What? What is it?"

Ailill only stared at us, while Louis and Aidan shifted and followed Moira's lead. They'd failed to heed my warnings before, to the detriment of us all. Louis even pushed his chair back and climbed to his feet.

But people were milling about, and I thought the young white man with the wild dark hair and wilder eyes was headed for the bathroom. Until his hand was on Moira's shoulder, his aura of hope nearly suffocating me.

"Is it you?" He had a voice like a snake, but his hope felt genuine, even as he dramatically fell to his knees behind Moira's chair. His eyes darted between me and Moira. I felt oddly exposed. "Or is it you?"

"Hey!" Aidan called, pulling the stranger's hand off Moira, and Louis darted forward to pull the boy back.

The lad shuffled around on his knees to squeeze between Moira's and my chairs.

"What do you think you're doing?" Louis demanded, tugging on the stranger's arm.

"You have to help me," the boy said, freeing his limbs from Louis and Aidan.

Ailill only stared, astonished. And Moira didn't look frightened. There was no question we were both thinking of the same thing: The old woman who had shown up at Bunrowan begging for my help. She'd wailed about something called the frenzy and even addressed me as "great queen." She'd said I could heal "that which I caused" and admitted to seeing and hearing things that weren't there. And now a second stranger appeared out of nowhere, seeking my help? This was no coincidence.

Moira glanced at me, and I shook my head, letting her know this boy didn't feel like a threat.

"Is he drunk?" Aidan asked, breaking the boy's grip every time he found purchase on Moira's or my arms. "He's not in his right mind."

"I am!" the boy cried in Aidan's face. He turned back to Moira, his hope morphing into desperation as tears bloomed in his eyes. "Please, it's not an ailment of the mind! It's not the Morrigu I need!"

At the name, everyone at our table went still.

"Macha, which of you is Macha? It's my lungs. I know you're the eternal mother, Macha. You can heal the body. They've told me that. *She* told me that."

Moira and I stared at one another.

"Who? Who says that?" Louis demanded.

The anguish from the young man was strangling me. He didn't

even turn to Louis as he whispered, "Medb."

"Okay, time for you to go," Louis muttered, hauling the boy up by the arm.

"No!" the boy yelled, but Louis wasn't messing about this time, and his grip was fast. The boy's foot connected with a nearby table, sending it flying.

"Oi!" A shout came from across the bar as Aidan joined the tussle.

"No, no, no!" the boy was crying. "I know Macha is here! I saw the *ollam*'s hound outside!"

"What's going on here?" It was the barman, back again and twice as mad. "Fightin'? There's no fightin' in my pub!"

"We're not—" Aidan's protest died as the boy sized up the irate bartender and dashed for the door.

We watched him go in astonishment. Moira squeezed my hand.

"Out!" The bartender shouted, righting the table that had been knocked over. "Ye are too much trouble. Get out!"

teacht le chéile
REUNION

b r í d

My legs shook so badly, I nearly tripped on the steps to Ráth da Dtarbh as I scurried back to safety. Finbar squawked, his wings thumping against the bars of the cage in a futile attempt to take flight. These people had captured my Finbar and locked him away in a cage. They'd hidden the other half of my soul from me. It had been Medb's doing, there was no question. But did Fenora know about this? I faltered at the threshold. I couldn't bear the thought that Fenora had been in on it. That she'd known, all along, where my Finny had been. After I had introduced her to him, told her what he meant to me. The force of the potential betrayal took my breath away.

"Don't!" Finbar screeched, but the word broke, as if he were getting reaccustomed to using his voice.

The sound staked my heart, and each of the bars of his cage began to bend with the force of my shaking hands, the wind in my veins in a

fury. Finbar stuck his head between the widening gap between two bars, and I shouted out as my rage piqued, rending the cage in two.

Finbar swooped into the sky.

Panting, I slumped to the ground, my back against the house, and flung the tangle of metal away from me. My whole body shook with the effort of it. *How did I do that?*

Something whispered back: *You didn't. The wind did.*

"Finny," I called, scared. "Come here!" I was being a little too loud, too angry and tired and confused and lost to consider what I would do if any of the girls sleeping inside the roundhouse woke up. If Fenora woke up.

But Finny was wheeling away from me. He doubled back and flew low to peck at my feet, and then swooped away again.

I didn't begrudge him the need to stretch his wings and fly after being locked up, but at the moment, I just wanted to clutch him against me, feel the scratch of his feet on my shoulder. He did it again— doubling back and swooping to peck at my feet, before taking to the sky again. And then I got it: he wanted me to follow him.

I didn't think twice. I simply dashed down the stairs after him.

He glided effortlessly down the street, reveling in the wind beneath his wings. I wondered again whether he wasn't just enjoying himself, making up for lost time in the sky, but he turned his head back to look for me more than once, confirming what I suspected—he wanted to show me something.

Maybe he'd discovered a way out, and Medb had noticed, and that was why she'd caged him. And now I was mere moments away from stepping back into my world. The woolen dress felt heavy on my shoulders, the boots cumbersome on my feet. What a sight I would be stumbling back into the real world with a great fluffy fur around my shoulders!

But Finbar cut right, toward Ráth Cruachan.

My heart sputtered. Why were we going back there?

But he didn't make for the stairs, which were still dotted with people stumbling and merry with drink. Instead, he twisted around and headed toward the back of the mound, where I'd climbed to the kitchens and found him. Trying not to bring attention to myself, I dashed after him, crouching behind the fence when the guards at the door to Medb's house turned in my direction. Finbar looped back around to wait for me and then flew on.

We passed around the field at the back of the hill, and the drone of the bees felt oddly comforting. As Finny swooped back around to the other side, I realized where we were headed. In my search for Finbar, I'd come here several times—the barred wall of the cell where I'd first been held.

"Finny, what are we doing?" I mumbled under my breath.

Sure enough, Finbar swooped low toward the cell I could identify as my own thanks to the small bit of bog asphodel that Fenora had planted outside it. He flew a bit farther and then alighted on the ground, looking back at me intently. It was another barred wall set with a door into a dark cave. How many cells were carved into the earth below Ráth Cruachan?

Advancing slowly, mostly to catch my breath, I glanced around to make sure nobody was around. There was a door to the house on this side of the complex too, but the guards were up at the top of the stairs, and I was sure the dark was enough to hide me all the way down here near the earth.

Taking a deep breath, I crouched down beside Finbar and peeked around the corner into the dark cell. "What are we here for, Finny?"

In the murky light from the moon, I could see a cell quite like the one I'd found myself in. Leaning closer, I grasped the bars with my hands and squinted. Crumpled in one corner was a thin figure. Finbar squawked and pecked at my hand, making the figure stir.

"Hush!" I hissed, extending a finger for Finbar to hop onto. He obliged but twisted his head, like he couldn't understand me right now.

The figure climbed unsteadily to its feet. It was a man in a rumpled shirt and trousers, his feet bare. He moved erratically, like something essential was broken, but headed steadily toward us.

Only when he stepped into the moonlight streaming through the bars did I recognize his dirty, pallid face.

"Dad?"

"Hush! Hush!" Finbar squawked at me. He pecked at my fingers and flapped his wings.

"Bríd?" Dad's eyes widened in his dirt-streaked face. "Bríd, what are you doing here?"

I squeezed my arms through the bars as far as they would go, clutching my dad's arms. They were thin and cold. "Are you hurt? We have to get you out of here!"

Dad shook his head, and guilt flipped my stomach. He'd been here all along, and what had I been doing? Dancing with silly boys and a dour princess. When I could have been saving my family. Moira would have been ashamed of me.

"Bríd," he hissed, his voice low as he glanced over my shoulders at the deserted street beyond, "you need to leave. Leave Cruachan now."

Everything Medb had told me about my sisters, my father, and my life came pouring over me. "Dad, she told me you gave us up! She said you traded our safety for money. That's how they found us. And when you didn't come back—"

"No." Dad was shaking his head, his eyes glistening, and grabbed my hand. "That's not what happened, Bríd."

"But—"

"My dear girl, you need to leave," he begged, his eyes constantly watching the street behind me. "Don't lose yourself here. Don't let her lies take root."

Hastily wiping my eyes, I tried to conquer the wind that was building in me. "Then what am I supposed to believe?"

"I am sorry I failed you and your sisters," Dad said sternly. "And I swear to you that everything will be clear when you're older." He squeezed my hand. His palms were cold. "But you need to *get out*."

"I'm not going anywhere without you. You need to tell me how to get you out of here."

"She only has me here to attract you girls. Go home, *now*."

Guilt returned with a vengeance.

Home. How could I tell him? That everything he and Mam had built for us was gone? Because of me. Because I hadn't had the guts to tell my sisters what I'd seen in my dreams and had instead lied to the *bean nighe.*

"And as soon as you get home," he went on, wiping a tear from my cheek with his thumb, "you need to get your things together and leave

Ireland. Go to Canada. Or the US or Australia. Somewhere far away."

"What? Dad, stop speaking nonsense—"

"*Hé! Cé atá thíos ansin?*"

Pulling away from the bars, I looked frantically around. The two guards at the top of the mound were shuffling down the stairs, squinting in my direction.

"Feck! I swear to you, Dad, I will get you out of here," I said, squeezing his hands tightly. "And then I will repay her for this. For what she's done to you, what she's done to Ríona and Moira."

Dad closed his eyes. "Bríd, no—"

"I will make her wish she was never born," I cried through my tears. "And then I will kill her."

"Awk! Kill! Kill!" Finbar squawked.

"Hey! Hey, you," the guard called. They were on the road now, making their way toward us.

"Finny, you have to stay with him," I whispered, my voice shaking. "Hide yourself nearby and watch him. Please."

"Kill," Finbar squawked before launching himself from my shoulder. With one last glance at my dad's helpless face, pale in the moonlight, I turned, lifted my skirts, and ran.

costas na draíochta

THE PRICE OF MAGIC

moira

We slept on the boat that night. Aidan, Ríona, and I were tucked into the cabin with some slightly musty blankets Ailill had retrieved from an old trunk. Through the window, I could see Louis on watch, sitting in the grass of the quay near Bó, Conry sprawled out beside them. Ailill was perched on the deck of the boat, also "on watch," but his snores gave him away. I needed to sleep so that we could swap stations in a few hours and Louis could get some sleep. But the knowledge that I was the one marked with the Blood Omen and the memory of that boy's pleas combined to keep me awake.

The cabin was a tight squeeze for three of us plus a wolf. Faolan lay curled between me and Ríona, and I was grateful for his warmth. I'd done Ríona's hair for bed and then she'd fallen right to sleep, like our old ritual was an immense comfort. Foregoing braids tonight, I'd gently stretched and twisted her curls into a bun and wrapped it all in Mam's

yellow satin scarf. Now she lay with her hands slipped under her chin, the picture of peace. On my other side, Aidan lay flat on his back, staring at the ceiling.

"You're not sleeping," I said.

He grinned and turned his head to look at me. His eyes shone warmly in the moonlight. "Neither are you."

"Not yet," I said, sighing deeply.

Aidan tentatively reached out, gently touching my hand. I let him take it in his. We lay like that, curled toward each other, hand in hand, for a long while. My eyelids began to feel heavy, and I felt the soft, happy anticipation of sleep.

"Do you think you really can heal people?" Aidan whispered.

I was instantly awake. Of course, I knew he'd been ill—that was why he'd taken to his seal form all those years ago—and that maybe it was possible he would be sick again one day. I understood what he was hoping. But I couldn't bear for those hopes to hinge on me. Me and this truly unbelievable fantasy.

"I don't think so," I murmured.

He pressed his lips together and looked at the ground. With his free hand, he tugged at a thread in the tatty quilt wrapped around him.

"Don't you think I would have known by this point in my life if I had that kind of power?" I whispered.

Aidan shrugged, his cheeks flushing. He was embarrassed. I had the urge to reach out and hug him, but my courage failed.

"When we saw that old wise-woman on Inis Mór," Aidan whispered, licking his lips, "she said . . . well, she had me touch this, this vial. And then she told me I'm still sick. The selkie thing, going back to the sea . . . it didn't work."

It was suddenly freezing cold in the little cabin, and I squeezed his hand. "Why didn't you tell me?"

Aidan shrugged. "I didn't intend to tell anyone, and Ríona seemed on board to keep my secret. But . . . well, I don't know. I guess that guy coming to the pub tonight, it made me think maybe you could do those things they say. Maybe you could help me." He shook his head. "It sounds stupid now."

Faolan gave an annoyed huff and rolled over, nestling away from me and toward Ríona. Aidan gave a weak smile and closed his eyes, as if to say, *Let's forget it and go to sleep.* He sighed and curled his free hand under his cheek.

"I'll try," I whispered.

His eyes flew open. "What?"

"We don't even know if I'm Macha. It could be Bríd. But I'll . . . I'll try." Taking a deep breath, I sat up.

Something like alarm flashed across Aidan's face. "Now?" he asked breathlessly.

I shrugged, thinking of how helpless I'd felt on this journey. How I'd never managed to purposely conjure a curio, despite everyone's belief in our magic. "I'd like to know," I said softly. "We have to come up with a new plan when we leave here tomorrow. It might help to know if I'm really capable of . . ." I finished the sentence with another weak shrug.

Real powerful, Moira.

Aidan sat cross-legged and faced me. I glanced over my shoulder to check that Ríona was still asleep. Faolan opened one eye to see what we were up to before sighing and going back to sleep.

"I trust you," Aidan whispered. His voice was husky.

I took a deep breath and squared up to face him. "Okay, what do you think I do?" We sat with our knees touching. He seemed to be shaking a bit, but I wasn't entirely sure it wasn't my own body shaking his.

"I don't know," he whispered. "Do you have any idea how you made the curios?"

I shook my head. "We just sort of . . . wanted things, and they happened." After another deep, steadying breath, I grabbed both his hands and held them firmly in my own, focusing on the pressure of his skin against mine. Then I closed my eyes and hoped. Wanted. Wished.

With all my heart, I wished that this boy was healthy and happy and uninjured and without pain. Thinking these things choked my throat with emotion, but I took deep breaths to focus on the truth: *I want Aidan to be healthy. I want the disease he's struggled with gone forever.*

Nothing happened.

For the longest moments of my life, nothing happened. My cheeks began to burn, and tears welled in my eyes. Not just from the frustration that I couldn't heal Aidan but from the embarrassment of thinking maybe this would work, and above all, *wanting* it to work. Wanting to be special.

And then the boat shook. It was a quick shudder, like a particularly big wave had knocked it sideways. But there were no waves here on the Liffey.

Faolan and Ríona both jumped up, bleary-eyed and breathing heavily. Outside, Ailill shouted, shaken out of his slumber. Aidan stared at me.

"What was that?" Louis shouted to Ailill, his voice muffled from shore.

Still, Aidan stared at me.

"How . . . how will we know if it worked?" I breathed.

"Moira? Ríona?" Louis's call was hesitant. "You might want to come out here."

Not meeting Ríona's eyes, I stepped outside, the others on my heels. Louis and Ailill stood looking over the side of the boat. Their faces showed astonishment, with a hint of trepidation, as we joined them there and looked down into the water.

The mucky green water was thick with dead fish. A thin ring of pale bellies lined the boat. The water beyond was clear. Before anyone could say anything, there was a thump, and we all turned to find a seagull, dead on the deck.

"Um, Moira?" Aidan said, his voice shaking. "I think it worked." With a shaking hand, he pulled up his pant leg and ran a palm over his shin. The angry red aftermath of the battle at Bunrowan was now just a shiny scar. Without meeting my gaze, he lifted his shirt to reveal the patch of stomach where the kelpie had wounded him. The wound was completely gone.

There was horror in his eyes when they finally met mine. Gulping, he looked from the seagull to the fish and back to me. Ríona shook like a leaf beside me.

"You did this?" Ailill asked, crossing his arms over his chest. His gaze was heavy on me. I wanted to cry.

"I . . . I think so." And what of Aidan's illness? Had that part worked? And if it had . . . what life had been the cost?

I was going to vomit. I was suddenly sure of it.

Ailill looked from me to the dead fish and back. "You three are a menace to society wandering 'round with no knowledge of who ye are or where ye come from," he said, dragging a hand over his face. "I'll take you to Cruachan. I'm not saying I'll do battle for you. But I'll go." The perfect white form of the dead seagull shone in the moonlight. Ailill shook his head. "I'll go. For the sake of Ireland."

feall
BETRAYAL

brid

"What's on the agenda today, Fenora?"

There was a pause, and I could imagine the pained look on Fenora's face. She wouldn't know how to answer the girl. But I couldn't see her face to confirm my assumptions. I was curled into myself, still beneath the heavy fur blanket on my bed, turned away from the other girls. I didn't want them to see the tear tracks down my face. Or the bags under my eyes. Not yet. I hadn't thought of an excuse for them yet. Nor an excuse for why I'd been making a fuss in the kitchen.

But nobody had said anything yet. Nobody had come for me in the night. Had the kitchen girls really told no one? Had Medb not noticed the cage was gone? Maybe I needed to pay for the girls' silence. Or maybe it was already too late. Perhaps they'd already told and Medb kept her silence for some greater play that was yet to come . . .

"I'm not sure," Fenora said, and I imagined she might have been

looking at me. For some signal. After all, I'd promised her, hadn't I? I'd promised her we would run away and find my sisters and go somewhere safe. Together. She thought this was going to be the biggest day of her life. And she couldn't tell the other girls about it.

But that promise had been made yesterday. When the sun had dawned today, I had a plan, that was still true. But it was quite a different plan. One that didn't involve Fenora.

After all, what if Fenora had known? All along? That my father was her mother's prisoner? There was no way I could know, no question I could ask that would guarantee the truth. Because Medb was right—I was alone here. Well and truly alone. I couldn't trust anyone from here on out.

That's what I'd decided while not sleeping the night before. Sleep was difficult when you were planning the downfall of a feckin' centuries-old evil queen. But it was what I had to do. The greatest threat to my family right now was Medb herself. I didn't know who would gain power if Medb were to die, but it would certainly cause turmoil, and it was in that turmoil that I intended to rescue my father and get us both out of here.

Fenora didn't factor into that. Fenora *couldn't* factor into that. Not when it was her own mother I was up against.

The girls chattered away as they moved about the room, dressing and preparing for the day. I felt a presence beside my bed and thought about pretending to be asleep a little longer. My heart flipped at the memory of Fenora's face yesterday as her mother had declared a ruthless challenge that would change her life forever.

Did she know? Did she know Finbar and my father were locked up this whole time? I suddenly wanted to see her face. As though that would tell me the answer.

Feigning a yawn, I turned over and acted surprised to see Fenora standing there uncertainly. "Good morning," I said softly.

"*Dia dhuit ar maidin*," Fenora said with a shy nod. She looked uncertain whether last night had been a dream, or if a simple night's sleep had cured me of my notions of running away with her.

I sighed. The night had cured me of many things indeed.

Over her shoulder, I saw a tiny shadow hop into the doorway. *Finbar.* He saw me looking, cocked his head, and hopped right back out of sight. Of course he was checking up on me. That came as naturally to him as flying. I didn't mind, as long as he flew straight back to keep watch over Dad.

Forcing a smile onto my face, I turned back to Fenora. "Another day of feasting?"

"My . . . my mother wishes to see you," Fenora said uncertainly. "She says she wishes to show you off to the Ulster party."

A frisson of fear ran through me, and I lifted my chin. "Wonderful."

Fenora's brow furrowed. "Really?"

I swung my legs over the side of the bed. "Of course."

Fenora nodded slowly. "She does like you," she said slowly. "I hope that's . . . helpful."

Helpful indeed. I didn't have any weapons. Nor any real idea of Medb's vulnerabilities. But that was something I would find out. Fenora had said it herself. They weren't invincible. And I already had the advantage I needed:

They like me, I thought with some satisfaction. *They like me, and that will be their downfall.*

uaimh na gcat
CAVE OF THE CATS

ríona

"I'm not going in there," Moira said simply. She'd been snappish since the incident on the boat. The dead creatures, which she claimed had been her own doing in an attempt to heal Aidan, had marred her heart. Everything I'd felt from her since then had been sad, bitter, dark . . . hopeless. And hope was something we couldn't afford to lose right now.

"Come on. We need to hide out in *Uaimh na gCat* until we have a plan," Louis explained for the thousandth time. One didn't need to be the Morrigu to be able to tell that he was nervous. On the journey here, he'd kept repeating instructions and recalling Conry to his side when the hound had strayed too far. He and Ailill had agreed this cave near Cruachan was where we would set up camp while we plotted.

When he'd first brought it up, I was shocked to realize I'd heard of it before. *"They say it's where you—or rather, the goddess—first crawled out of*

the Otherworld." That's what old Biddy Nolan on Inis Mór had told me.

Our tired group stood in a muddy field before the entrance to the infamous cave. It was nothing more than a small, dark gash in the earth. You'd have to get on your hands and knees to slither inside. Which was precisely what Ailill had told us to do.

"We can't linger here," Ailill hissed, his gaze roving around behind us. "Tie the mare behind the tree there and get inside. Best to go in on your bum now, come along."

A huge hawthorn towered over the entrance, its prickly branches making the prospect of climbing inside even more menacing. But Ailill was radiating fear and Louis looked scared—which meant I wasn't underestimating our situation. With one last glance at Moira, who had indignation rising in her, ready to protest one more time, I stepped forward and dropped to the ground. My fingers squelched in mud as I scooted into the darkness on my backside. Faolan was just behind me.

Inside was a small space with barely enough room for another person. I heard Moira's annoyed grumblings outside as she was forced to leave Bó yet again. "Why are you so scared?" she asked Louis.

Louis gave a little laugh. "Well, let's just say it's not my first time going through the Gate to Hell."

"You can't call it that and expect me to go waltzing right in!" Moira shrieked.

Conry was in next, followed by Louis. As he turned to motion for Moira to join us, I studied the lintel stone above the entrance. There was an inscription there in ogham script. The ancient marks of ogham could be found on many stones across Ireland, but I'd never seen them in person before. The message would have been in the early Irish language.

"We should head that way," Louis said, nodding toward the narrow passage branching off this chamber. "Make some room." Uneasy but determined, he headed for the passage, half crawling after Conry, who proceeded as slowly and carefully as his boy.

Taking a deep breath, I followed.

The dark got thicker as we moved, but the tunnel opened up a bit farther on, to the point that we could stand. It was damp down here, and the sound of dripping water was constant.

"Don't go any farther!" Ailill shouted from behind us.

There was a little light here, from what appeared to be a crack in the ceiling up ahead, so I could watch Louis as we waited. As always, it was unsettling for me not to be able to feel what he was feeling. But I could guess. His eyes darted around the stone walls, and he stood folded in on himself, his arms crossed over his chest. His hand was knotted firmly in Conry's fur.

Faolan gave a soft whine as I shifted my weight from foot to foot. Moira's hand slipped into mine the second she reached us, Aidan just behind her.

"Do you feel at home?" Ailill asked, breath heaving as he caught up with us and clumsily got to his feet. The light struck his face at an angle, making him look older.

"No," Moira snapped. "Why?"

I hadn't told her. In my rush to relay everything Biddy had told us when we returned to the mainland, I'd forgotten to tell Moira about the Morrigan and the Otherworld.

"Uaimh na gCat," Ailill said. "Oweneygat. Home of the Morrigan."

Moira gaped at him.

"You have to be kidding," Aidan muttered.

Ailill shook his head. "The Cave of the Cats. The Gate to Hell. This is the door to the Underworld. The door the Morrigan used to travel back and forth."

"And site of many a hazing ritual for the warriors of Cruachan," Louis said darkly. "I'd like to limit my time here as much as possible."

"Hazing?" Ailill scoffed. "It's just a rite of passage, lad."

"The Gate to Hell?" Aidan repeated breathlessly.

"Arah, that name was used just by the Christians, weren't it?" Ailill said with a shrug.

Moira interrupted. "Why are we here?"

"We need a place near Cruachan to hide out and gather ourselves, and this is perfect," Ailill explained. "But you mustn't go any farther into the passage. Just beyond this point, where it narrows down there"—he pointed to the end of the passage—"that's where it opens up to the cave itself. That's where the entrance to the Otherworld is. You're not ready for that. So don't go past this point."

"Not sure we'll ever be ready for that," Moira muttered, squeezing my hand.

"Now," Ailill said gravely. "First, I am going to take you into Cruachan—"

"You're going to do what?" Louis thundered.

"They have to see what they're up against with their own eyes," Ailill said. "We'll enter at the back, near the well, and stay hidden. Then we'll come back here and regroup."

Louis shook his head, and Conry gave a displeased snort. But the pair didn't look too keen on staying here in the cave either.

"Fine," Louis muttered at last. "But everyone must keep their heads down, and we speak to no one."

"This is our meeting point," Ailill added. "Any trouble, and you come straight back here."

"Straight back to the Gate to Hell?" Aidan asked helplessly.

"What kind of trouble?" Moira asked. The deep, dark hopelessness I'd been feeling from her was starting to sprint into fear.

"There's not much of the expected in Cruachan," Ailill said, the ghost of a smile on his lips. "But you can always expect trouble."

AILILL brought us to an empty field. There were grassy mounds dotting the landscape, which stretched on like any stretch of farmland in Ireland. And though I didn't want to admit it to myself, much less to anybody else, I thought I could hear people talking. Somewhere out of sight, a sheep bleated, though I couldn't see any animals around the place, which was odd in and of itself.

Ailill stood there, taking a deep breath, as if we were merely waiting for a train. "Line up," he said, gesturing at a ditch running along the edge of the field. "Louis and I will be able to cross ourselves, but the three of ye, you'll need a little . . . push."

Moira and I exchanged a glance but obediently stepped up to the ditch. We both felt bare and alone with Bó and Faolan left back at the cave. Even Conry had been ordered to stay, being "the most recognizable hound in Cruachan," according to Louis.

Moira's hand slipped into mine, and she took one of Aidan's, too, as she stepped up to the ditch.

"Ye ready?" Ailill asked. His pale, misty aura had turned solid and bright. He was on a mission.

"Remember," Louis said, "don't speak to anyone."

Ailill whispered something before a sharp shove between my shoulder blades sent me sprawling.

When I looked up, I was kneeling on the edge of a city. No, not a city exactly. More like a country town, stretching as far as the eye could see. There weren't many people near us, just a ramshackle structure with smoke coiling out of its roof. But a lane ran from where we stood down into a warren of primitive roundhouses and foot traffic, mostly people with carts and horses and cows. Each deserted mound we'd been staring at moments before was now a fortified dwelling with extensive structures atop and people moving up and down the incline. I could faintly sense the feelings and auras of strangers wafting toward us. Had we gone back in time?

Ailill and Louis stepped carefully over the ditch behind us, looking quite adept at this form of . . . transportation.

"Welcome to Cruachan," Ailill said, his eyebrows low. "Trust no one."

"This is her city?" Moira asked, as she helped me to my feet. Aidan sprang to his, any injuries only a memory. "This is where Medb lives?"

"Aye," Ailill muttered. "We'll only gawk a few minutes, and we'll stick to the shadows. The ring road will be crowded the closer to her rooms we get."

Sure enough, as we moved behind the nearest roundhouses, the feelings bombarded me. Excitement, contentment, sadness, desperation—they mingled and twisted together in that heady rush that always hit me when we went into town back home. It made me unsteady on my feet, and I reached out for Moira's hand.

Astonishment permeated her every pore. The sounds of living had grown louder. Dogs, kids shouting, metal clanging on metal. Between buildings and ramshackle sheds, we spotted cats slinking and people walking here and there, talking, wrangling kids or animals, going about life. Right here in an invisible city in Roscommon. And the people. They dressed like it was another century, sure, but this place was more diverse than Galway city. I watched a Black girl with tight corkscrew curls heave a lamb from one hip to the other as she lugged him down the road.

"I wouldn't dare go any farther," Ailill whispered after we'd been walking only a minute. He was alert but confident. A steady aura of sharp concentration. I could see how he'd been a royal guard.

"How do we find out where to look for Bríd and our father?" Moira asked. "This place is massive."

Louis's gaze was on one of the great mounds, still quite a distance away. But Ailill's eyes were transfixed on the doorway to a roundhouse perched on the nearest mound. A heavy sadness hung on him. This particular place meant something to him.

I studied the roundhouse. It was plain and rather short, but there was nothing to mark it as special. A pair of girls walked inside, arm in arm, as we watched.

We hadn't been standing there even half a minute when Ailill shook his head and said, "We should go."

"Did you hear that?" Aidan asked. We turned to look at him. He was standing close to the nearest hut, and sure enough, you could hear a couple of lads speaking inside.

"Don't waste your time," one said.

"You think it takes some kind of skill to hunt down a powerless traitor?" another asked. "I'll have the *ollam* killed before you're even out of Cruachan."

We all looked at Louis.

"Lú is more powerful than she lets on," the first boy said. "She must make him seem weak to rile us up, to get us to go after him."

"You're treading awfully close to treason."

Ailill shook his head and muttered, "It's time to go." Without another glance at Cruachan, he turned and walked back in the direction we'd come from.

"Louis," Moira asked, grabbing Louis's arm to stop him from escaping after Ailill. "Why are they hunting you?"

"I don't know," Louis murmured. "But I have a few good guesses." His face had gone as white as morning fog.

That was when I saw him. No, *felt* him. In the open doorway of the roundhouse Ailill had been staring at. A crow. Not just any crow, but a hooded crow who turned and hopped across the grass, squawking, "*Abeg! Feck!*" all the way. His feelings pricked at me, tiny stabs of irritation.

Moira was staring too. "She's here."

"*Abeg*," Finbar said, taking to the sky, completely oblivious to his audience.

bláthanna an phortaigh
FLOWERS OF THE BOG

bríd

I ate their food. I danced with their men. I even picked up the *bodhrán* and began to learn how to accompany the poems and songs her mother forced her to learn and recite at any given moment. The histories of Ireland.

And Fenora. Fenora watched me carefully, waiting, I knew, for any sign from me that we would do what we'd planned—run away together. So, I merely avoided her gaze and ensured we were never alone.

Still, nobody said anything about Finbar. Either the kitchen girls hadn't told Medb and she hadn't discovered that the cage was gone . . . or she knew and she was waiting for me to do something stupid. Which I wasn't going to do. I was going to pretend everything was fine.

I didn't dare go back to see Dad either. They couldn't know that I knew. I needed them to believe I was comfortable here. Enjoying

myself. Feeling at home. At home in this court of Medb's. I needed all of them to believe it. Even Fenora. So that when I finally had time to put my plan into action, nobody would expect it. Only, there were a few parts of that plan that still needed figuring out.

In the meantime, there was much desperation and many declarations of love from the other girls in Ráth da Dtarbh, as many of the boys of Cruachan and even some of the Ulster party geared up and moved out to hunt Louis. I thought of sending Finbar to warn him, but I couldn't spare Finbar at the moment. He was my only contact with Dad.

Medb planned a halfhearted attempt to continue the festive atmosphere as men left Cruachan. She organized a day for the girls to go looking for *fraochán*, or bilberries. The shrubs would be full of fruit now, and the best treat in the world was apparently a bowl of bilberries with fresh honey. There was no way it was going to be as delicious as the coconut candy my mother used to make, but I went along with them anyway.

The trek to the hills on the edge of Cruachan was unremarkable. Medb hadn't come herself, but she'd sent along one of the girls who worked in the kitchen to carry the baskets. I realized with a start that this girl, whom they called Mary, had been in the kitchen last night when I'd stolen back Finbar. I watched her carefully, to see if she looked at me strangely or pointedly avoided me.

"Bríd, I see a shrub just there quite heavy with fruit," Fenora said, interrupting my study of the kitchen girl. Fenora twisted the empty basket in her hands, watching me with a bit of trepidation. "Would you come along with me?"

The girl named Úna, often picked on by Medb when she was trying to punish Fenora, was standing nearby. I thrust out an arm and threaded it through Úna's. "Wonderful find, Fenora. Úna was just saying she's feckin' famished. Come with us, Úna."

Poor Úna looked completely confused but didn't protest. She was accustomed to being used.

Fenora looked crestfallen. It wasn't the first time I had rather obviously avoided being alone with her. I just didn't know what I would say to her if she asked about our plan to run away together.

I had a different plan now.

And it was at that moment, standing on the grassy hillside picking bilberries with the other girls, that the last piece of the plan fell into place.

It was the kitchen girl, Mary, who first bent to pick an upright green plant with bright, skinny leaves and took a bite.

"What's that?" I asked her, in order to study how she'd react to me. To try and ascertain where we stood.

"Bitter cress," she said, twisting the stem in her fingers. "This hill here is where we get all the sorrels for the kitchens. It has the best sun in the afternoon."

She gave no outward sign that she even recognized me from last night or remembered what had happened. But how could she not? I'd caused quite a stir. I'd be lucky if the commotion hadn't woken half the town. The way things had broken and furniture had moved when I'd gotten angry and the wind in my veins had grown into a storm . . . I didn't have an explanation for it. So, I hoped to any god there might be that she didn't ask for one.

Turning away from her, I looked out over the town. We were a bit above the streets here, and it gave quite a view over the lower end of Cruachan. I watched the people going about their daily lives down there in the small roundhouses that populated most of the town. I hadn't given much thought to their lives.

"There's much you can eat in the fields," Fenora said, stooping in the grass to run her fingers over a small fern-like plant. She picked a stem and held it out to me. "Sweet cicely. Try it, Bríd."

Guilt stirred in my stomach. She kept doing that—singling me out, trying to be friends.

"You know much about plants," Mary said to Fenora, impressed.

I accepted the stem and took a small bite. It was sweeter than I'd been expecting. A sly, wicked smile bloomed on Mary's face, and I was half-sure she was going to say something about last night.

But instead, she merely said, "Have ye ever had mushrooms? The special ones? Fly agaric, they're called. The red ones with the white spots. The Ulster lads brought some and shared them round."

Fenora rolled her eyes. Úna shook her head eagerly, eyes round.

"I can get ye some if ye like," Mary said. She knew she was scandalizing the esteemed princess and her friends. She watched Fenora for a long moment. "You needn't be all high and mighty," she said, rather bravely I thought. "The druids do them, you know."

"Yes, but you're not hanging around with druids, are you?" Fenora clenched her jaw. "You'll only get in trouble with those messers from Ulster."

"Mm, you think?" Mary asked. You could tell from the smirk on her face she wasn't afraid of Fenora and that her next words would be biting. "I guess you're one to know. You'll be marrying one of them soon enough."

Fenora glared at her. I wondered for a moment if she would do something rash—strike the kitchen maid, or simply scream at her. Instead, Fenora shook her head, her jaw set, and walked away.

Perhaps trying to break the awkward silence, Úna reached down to break a stem off a small shrub sprouting a cluster of tiny round flowers out the top. Each bloom hung on a pink stem, bent toward the ground. "This looks like a sweet," Úna said, plucking one of the bright pink blooms to toss into her mouth.

"No!" Mary shouted, grabbing Úna's hand.

Úna startled and jumped away from her.

"That's bog rosemary, that is," Mary scolded her. "Poisonous as snakes."

"What?" Úna threw the plant down and wiped her hands on her dress. "Are you joking?"

"A few too many of those and you'd be dizzy and choking for air." Mary shook her head, as though she thought Úna a true eejit. "Yer stomach would be wrecked. And then you'd be dead."

I knew bog rosemary. It grew in some wet areas near Bunrowan. But I'd seen it more recently than that. Yes, I'd seen it very recently.

The wind inside me stirred.

"Jaysus, be careful," Mary muttered, shaking her head.

I patted Úna on the back. "That's an easy mistake, to be sure," I said, smiling serenely. And then, turning to Mary, I added, "You must know all about these things, and how to prepare them in the kitchen. I'm hopeless with that. I'd love to help you sometime, to learn a thing or two."

Mary looked at me a little oddly but shrugged. "I s'pose we could always use an extra pair of hands."

strainséirí

STRANGERS

a i d a n

"Are you sure she's in Ráth da Dtarbh?" Louis asked yet again.

"If that's what you call that roundhouse we saw, then yes," Moira said, exasperated. "If Finbar is there, Bríd is there."

The dampness in the cave made me shiver. The others seemed immune to it. Conry was laid out on the floor, ruffing softly in his sleep. The hound truly slept more than any creature I'd ever met. Meanwhile, Faolan sat obediently at Ríona's side, ears perked. Poor Bó had been relegated, yet again, to a spot outside, behind the sprawling hawthorn.

Ríona bit her lip. She looked as if she knew Moira was being a bit too hasty, but what other options did we have? Sitting around watching the city sounded good to me, but it was only a matter of time before somebody noticed strangers hanging around. Or the two of us who weren't strangers. Somebody would recognize Ailill or Louis.

No, I knew we had to sneak into this roundhouse and see if that was where they were keeping Bríd. But we had to be careful about it.

"I think I should go alone," I said, stepping forward.

Ailill laughed out loud. My cheeks went red.

"What are you talking about?" Louis demanded. "You don't even know the city."

"You two would be recognized," I said.

"And you would be lost," Ailill said. "We have to go under the cover of night. You wouldn't be able to navigate the city without us."

"Then we all go," Moira said, "except Ríona. Ríona waits for us here."

Ríona stared at her sister, her mouth hanging open. Shaking her head, she furiously signed something to Moira.

"You are the one they want," Moira snapped back.

Ríona pressed her lips together and continued to argue, her hands flying. This time, Moira's face fell.

After a beat of silence, Louis sighed. "The Blood Omen? She's got you there."

Moira merely folded her arms over her chest.

The incessant sound of dripping water was the only thing to break the silence. I glanced around at my companions, wondering who would be the one to settle this.

"Lú and I will go to Ráth da Dtarbh with you," Ailill said, pointing at Moira. "You will stay here"—this to Ríona—"and the selkie will guard you."

"What?" I shouted.

Ríona looked livid.

"The Morrigu is safest here," Ailill said firmly. It was suddenly clear that he'd been a king. His tone brooked no argument. "One of the sisters must come with us, to identify their father should we stumble upon him. Therefore, you must guard the Morrigu."

Moira looked at me, pleading in her eyes. One glance at Ríona told me she was done arguing. She merely stared at the place where her fingers were twisted in Faolan's fur. Ailill waited several seconds to see if I'd argue. Finally, I nodded and looked at the ground.

"We go tomorrow," Ailill said. "After dark. Louis knows where we can source weapons."

Moira's face went even paler than usual, her freckles standing out. Ailill must have noticed, because he took a deep breath and looked at each of us for a long time.

"The games end here," he said. He turned to the sisters. "Ye will be risking your lives for your sister." Then he addressed me and Louis. "And ye will be risking your lives for a stranger." He waited for some kind of reaction from us, but we merely stared, shocked to hear the stakes laid out so plainly. "There is still time for you to decide that you are not willing to do that. For now. Once you leave this cave, it will be too late."

Stepping closer to Moira, I took her hand. Ríona was standing nearby, despondent. I took her hand, too, and Faolan sighed deeply, as if in relief. These people weren't strangers anymore. Squeezing the sisters' hands, I said, "I'm willing."

Louis grabbed Ríona's free hand and nodded. "Me too."

Ailill considered us a moment longer. He nodded. "Then rest up. Tomorrow will be here too soon."

comhréiteach déanta i ndomlas

A TRUCE MADE IN BILE

bríd

By the next morning, I could tell Mary was a valuable ally.

While the other girls were getting dressed and halfheartedly preparing for the day, I'd slipped out to the kitchen on Ráth Cruachan. There, I'd found Mary and a few other girls who were working the meals for Medb's rooms that day, which they apparently did every day. They shuffled around cleaning up the messy countertops and harvesting things from the garden, the drone of bees filling the room through the open doorway. They told me the cook, who liked to give out to them for every small thing, and made them work silently, wouldn't be in until closer to dinner. Until then, they had free rein, their only real obligation being to respond to and fulfill Medb's occasional whim.

And they took their liberty freely. They contributed to the mess

almost as much as they tidied up. And their gossip revolved around Fenora and her stuck-up housemates, when they didn't think I could hear them, and when they weren't chittering about this visiting boy from Ulster or that one. I had to stop myself from defending Fenora more than once. That wasn't why I was here. Let them think what they would of Queen Medb's daughter. I didn't even know what *I* thought of her anymore. But none of that was relevant. I was here for one reason only.

That morning, I'd come only with the intention of reconnaissance. So, I asked questions about the cook's schedule. I found the mortar and pestle on a shelf at the back of the kitchen. I wondered aloud about Medb's eating habits.

And then I saw Mary stirring the mead.

"Do you make the mead yourselves, like?" I asked as Mary dropped sliced apples and fresh bilberries into the barrel.

"Arah, no," she said, licking a finger that ran with fruit juice. "The lads over on An Ráth Mór take care of that. But we dress it up the way the queen likes. All the fruits we can get our hands on and such. Why? That all you interested in learning to make?" She grinned and held out the big wooden spoon she was using to stir the mead.

"Actually," I said, putting on what I hoped passed for a smile despite the anxiety running through me, "I'm feeling a bit faint, j'know? I need to step outside for a moment."

Mary wrinkled her brow, but the ovens were on, so it was a fair enough excuse. I didn't mind if she thought me a weakling. Pretending to wipe my brow, I hurried out into the garden. I didn't let myself stop for a single moment. If I did, I was afraid my brain would reconsider.

And I was tired of considering. I needed to act.

There were two beekeepers in those frightful tunics tending the hives at the back of the garden, but they wouldn't be able to see what I was doing. The bog rosemary was down a row of wildflowers. It took me a minute to find it, but it was there, just as I'd remembered it. Kneeling in the grass, I looked furtively around. Nobody was paying me any mind. I started grabbing the rosemary out of the ground by the fistful. I wasn't sure which part of the plant was poisonous—maybe all of it—or how much I needed. I'd use as much as I could just to be sure.

"*Abeg*," I whispered to whatever gods were listening, the way my mother used to when she'd been at the end of her patience. *Abeg, please, let this work.*

"Abeg!" someone squawked behind me.

I jumped, dropping two fistfuls of green stems and bright pink flowers. Finbar hopped along the path toward me.

"Jaysus, Finny!" I gasped, making sure we'd attracted nobody's attention. Thankfully, the hives were too loud. "You scared the feckin' life out of me."

Finbar cocked his head at me and eyed the flowers I was frantically scooping up and dumping into the pockets of my borrowed dress. Talk about damning evidence. If Fenora got her hands on this dress, and this actually went according to plan, the culprit would be plain as day. But I didn't care. If it saved my sisters, it would be a success.

Finbar looked from the flowers to me, his shiny eyes round as marbles.

"This is none of your business," I said, plucking the last of the bog rosemary from the earth. Hopefully, nobody would notice this empty patch of earth until it was too late. "I need you to go watch Dad."

Climbing to my feet, I stumbled back toward the kitchen. When I glanced over my shoulder, Finbar was still hopping along after me.

"Go!" I hissed. "Please!"

Finbar stopped and cocked his head at me again. I glanced at the kitchen. We were close enough that if he started chattering now, the girls would hear.

"*Abeg*, Finny," I hissed, tears welling in my eyes.

He hopped twice and took to the air, making a big loop around the garden before disappearing over the side of the roundhouse.

Taking a deep, steadying breath, I turned back to the kitchen. As I stepped into the warm, dim space, Mary and the other girls fell silent. They'd been talking about me then.

Let them.

"Would you keep this moving for a moment more?" Mary asked, holding the wooden spoon out to me. "I need to get the tray prepared."

It was almost too easy. Mary scurried away into another room, and the other girls had turned away, trying extra hard not to pay me any mind, probably to cover the fact that they'd been gossiping about me. That made it easy to swipe the mortar and pestle off the shelf.

The wind in my veins whirling dangerously, I set about grinding the bog rosemary, dumping the resulting fine powder back in my pocket. I'd gotten through about half of my harvest when Mary returned to the kitchen with a tray and a small jug. I quickly started stirring the mead, shoving the pestle and mortar into the detritus of cooking supplies on the counter.

"Here we go," Mary said, setting down a tray and a big jug. "Would you fill that up there, and then I'll take it to the queen? I'll get some nuts too."

The minute she turned her back, I hastily filled the jug and dumped the powder in. All of it. Thankfully, it didn't change the color of the mead. The wind twisted and spun, beat inside my body like the wings of something fierce, as I furiously stirred the drink. My cheeks were as hot as fire pokers. Surely the girls could tell?

Mary reappeared. "Perfect, give it here now," Mary said, placing a small bowl of nuts beside the jug. "Let's add a bit more honey . . . The queen likes it sweet."

My limbs felt almost out of my control as Mary added a glob of honey to the mead and asked me to stir again.

When she finally slipped the tray from the table, I felt as if I might be carried away on the wind. I nearly called after her, to tell her to stop, to dump out the mead, but instead I said, "Shall I come with you?"

She was already through the door into the hall that led to Medb's rooms and just gave me a little shrug. Glancing around at the other girls, who still ignored me, I scurried after Mary.

Turning the last corner, we came face to face with two guards outside Medb's door. I must have visibly started. Mary looked at me strangely. "You best wait here," she said, knocking on the door. Without waiting for a reply, she stepped inside, closing the door behind her.

Giving the guards a friendly smile, hoping for all the world I looked like I belonged here, I waited. And listened. I could hear Medb's voice.

And then another. I tried to stop breathing, to listen harder. Yes, there was another voice. Not Mary's. Not Medb's. That meant . . . Medb wasn't alone.

What if the other people drank the mead? I hadn't even considered feckin' collateral damage.

Feck! Bríd, you eejit! Heart thumping, wind whipping into a funnel cloud in my gut, I took a few frantic steps toward the kitchen. I stopped. The guards would see me acting strangely. I couldn't *flee* right now. Oh Jaysus, what was I going to do?

Of course Medb wasn't feckin' alone.

Mary returned only a moment later, confusion on her face. She approached me where I stood awkwardly some distance from the guards, trying not to shift from one foot to the other.

"Medb's, uh, not alone, like?" I asked, my heart galloping in my chest. The wind was in such a frenzy, I felt like I was suffocating.

"She rarely is," Mary said slowly, narrowing her eyes at me. "She's entertaining today and requested a few extra bits for the girls."

"The girls? The girls are in there?" I asked. "Fenora and . . . the others?"

Mary narrowed her eyes at me. "They asked if I'd seen you. I had to say yes."

That morning, I'd scurried out of the roundhouse unseen . . . or so I had thought. But of course my absence would have been noticed eventually. Had Fenora's suspicions been piqued enough for her to say something to her mother? And perhaps she'd remembered me talking to Mary on our outing and thought to ask Mary what I was up to. The wind grew. I was in too deep. Now they knew I'd been in the kitchens.

If I were smart, I'd flee. Right this moment. Only, I didn't know how to get out of Cruachan.

And besides, I couldn't let any of the girls drink that mead.

Could I?

THE door creaked shut behind me. Medb sat in the chair nearest the fire, and Fenora was seated on the opposite side of the room, a few of the girls perched awkwardly between them. The tray was placed on a low table before Medb.

The room was too hot. I felt faint.

Medb nodded and said, "There you are. I'd heard you were missing."

Fenora's eyes were on me, but I didn't dare meet her gaze. Úna glanced around at the others before giving me a firm smile. As if she had to force herself to do it. Had they been talking about me in here too? Oh, how preferable the gossip of the kitchen girls was right now.

"Mary said you wanted to see me." At this point, that much truth wasn't going to get me in trouble. My eyes kept darting back to the tray, the mead, its jug perspiring in the heat, and I thought maybe I could make an excuse to take it with me when I left. If I could just make sure nobody drank from it before then.

"We were just discussing Fenora's prospects," Medb said, smiling serenely. "My daughter is a keener strategist than I would have thought."

"I would rather die a hermit than spend a single moment married to someone chosen by you," Fenora spat.

Medb nodded crisply. "Fiery words from someone who has never, in her miserable life, done a single thing to make her worthy of her title." Before Fenora could respond, Medb motioned at the tray on the table. "Help yourselves, *a chailíní*. Findabair's future won't be won on a sober stomach."

My insides were like a desert, the wind in me completely dead. I waited.

But nobody moved. Medb sat back in her chair, and the girls seemed to be frightened stiff, just like me. Fenora only crossed her arms and turned away from the group.

Thank feck. If I could just make an excuse to grab the tray and leave . . .

"Badb," Medb said, turning to me. Her smile was disarming. Not least of all because I knew from experience that it was a smile she would gladly wear as she locked up everyone I loved. Her gaze found mine and held it. "You've seen the lads leaving the city in the name of my great challenge. Do you not think it would be an honor to join in matrimony with a man who beat all others in such a feat of strength?"

Fenora scoffed. My cheeks flushed. If I looked at Fenora now, I would feel the need to defend her. "I'm afraid the marriage prospects of princesses are none of my business," I said instead.

"Indeed." Medb pursed her lips and looked at her daughter. "Well—" Whatever she would say next was interrupted.

"Úna, are you all right?" one of the girls whispered frantically.

Úna was bent over at the middle, clutching her stomach. I dashed forward, but she vomited, and I reared back. With a hand over her mouth, she fell to the floor.

My eyes found the object on the ground beside Úna. A wooden

cup lay on its side, empty but sticky with the residue of mead. I hadn't even seen her pour it.

"Úna?" Fenora was beside me as I tried to lift Úna into a sitting position. But her body fell limp as she lost consciousness, and I lost my grip. Her head *thunked* on the floor.

The girls screamed. Tears spilled down my cheeks, and I could barely breathe. The guards burst into the room among the chaos.

Medb hadn't moved from her chair. She looked from Úna to me. She was silent.

One of the girls was sobbing over Úna's body, the others screaming and tugging at her arms. The room was filling with guards. I could barely see through my tears and my breath felt trapped in my chest. I had to force it out. Fenora grabbed my arm, squeezing, and pressed her free hand to her mouth. "Is she . . . ?"

"She's merely fainted," Medb said. She was completely unfazed as she nodded to two of the guards. "Take her to the healer."

Two of the girls were beside themselves, their shrieks filling the air, and I couldn't get enough air into my lungs. We watched the guards lift Úna like she was nothing more than a rag doll and carry her from the room. When they were out of sight, leaving a handful of unsettled guards at the door, all eyes fell on Medb.

And Medb looked at me.

It felt like an eternity in the spotlight, tears leaving warm tracks down my cheeks, my chest heaving, before I realized Úna's empty cup was in my hand. I looked at it. It felt like my hand wasn't even attached to my body. When had I picked it up?

Medb stood, towering over me, and clasped her long fingers in front of her. "You shouldn't play games for which you are inadequately prepared, *a leanbh.*"

I felt apart from myself. Like the sobs wracking my body were coming from somebody else.

She knows. My breaths were loud, ripping from my chest. *Had Mary said something about me finding Finbar? Or was the guilt seeping off of me now enough for anyone in this room to put two and two together?*

"You, Badb, have become a little more trouble than you're worth." Medb shook her head and turned to the remaining guards. *"Déileáil léi."* *Deal with her.*

The guards' arms were on me before I could even process the command. The wind in my veins was uncontrollable. Something would happen, I was sure of it, just like when I'd found Finbar locked up in the kitchens. Something would happen—if only I could feckin' *breathe.* The snick of a short dagger being withdrawn from its sheath sounded behind me, and I gasped for air.

"No! Stop!"

It was Fenora. The cold touch of metal pressed against my throat but stopped there, waiting. Waiting to see if the queen would overrule the princess. Uncontrolled sobs came from the girls around us, but I didn't dare turn my head to look at them.

"Please!" Fenora cried again. Her blonde hair was tangled and frizzy over her shoulders, her tears falling onto her dress.

"Stop it, Findabair, you're embarrassing yourself and, more importantly, *me,*" Medb said. She stood calmly in the middle of the room, like a thwarted assassination attempt was all in a day's work.

"But you can't!" Fenora shouted. Her eyes darted to me and away. There was no breath left in me. I couldn't plead for my own life. So

Fenora was doing it for me. The other girls were crying harder now, holding each other. "You can't . . . kill her. She's all you have to attract the Morrigu."

My eyes flew to Fenora. Did that mean . . . did that mean she hadn't known Dad was here? She wasn't in on it with her evil mother?

Medb's eyes flashed dangerously. "You think she's all I have?" She scoffed. "You think I don't have other tools at my disposal? Other plans? Do you really believe that my power hinges on the whims of a teenage girl?"

The guard wielding the dagger shifted, and I gasped as the metal pressed against my skin.

"I'll do it!" Fenora yelped.

That, finally, gave Medb real pause. "Do what?"

"I'll marry the victor," Fenora said. "The winner of your ch-challenge. I'll m-marry whoever you wish, anyone who suits your agenda. I won't fight it, if you let her l-live." Fenora's eyes were wide with fear, the blue bright and watery.

The dagger eased off my neck even before I turned to see Medb's sinister smile.

"That, my dear Findabair, is a fair pledge."

The look on Medb's face when she finally met my eyes made it as clear as day: Somehow, I had played right into her plan. This entire day had gone exactly as she wanted. I'd been playing her game all along.

I had tried to kill Medb, Queen of Connacht, and I had failed. And now?

Medb nodded to the guard, who was already putting his dagger away. "Spare her. For now."

ag fanacht
WAITING

ríona

Turning, I paced down the length of the tunnel yet another time. Faolan had stalked back and forth with me for a little while, but now he realized the extent of our roaming was limited and he merely stood in the middle of the tunnel and watched me. Conry lay curled by the entrance to the tunnel, his ears pricked forward, and Bó was still tied up behind the big hawthorn tree last we'd checked. It felt like an extra layer of protection, having the True Mare watching over us. In reality, she'd be helpless to protect us in any meaningful way if we were discovered.

Which was why I didn't want to sit around here waiting to be found.

"You're going to wear a path in the stone," Aidan said, giving me a weak smile. His double energy, both sides of him tumultuous and frantic, belied the calm he was trying to project.

I clenched my jaw. The sound of dripping water drilled into my brain.

He shrugged. "Moira has this in hand. But they could be gone hours. You should rest."

Memories came flooding back to me. Every time Moira had ever stepped in front of a bully making fun of me or Bríd on the playground. Every time she had tried to make things better with one lash of her tongue. But these were things she couldn't fix so easily. We needed to fix them together.

My legs shaking, I marched back over to Aidan, nearly tripping over a rock in the process. I pulled my notepad out of my pocket. Towering over where he sat against the clammy wall of the cave, I scribbled down the one thought circulating in my head.

I want to go after them.

"No. Absolutely not," Aidan said, shaking his head. "The others were right. You are the one Medb wants. You can't go waltzing in there."

Exactly, I wrote. *I'm the one she wants. So I should be dealing with this.*

"Look," Aidan said, climbing to his feet. "I know it's painful to be stuck here while they go off on a daring mission. But I trust your sister more than anyone. And she wants you to stay here."

Pressing my lips together, I pocketed my notepad, turned away from him, and walked down the tunnel again. It wasn't worth arguing with him right now. Because I'd already decided. It took thirty seconds to walk down the length of the tunnel and back. Moira had one hour to get Bríd out of there and get safely back here.

Pacing the cave, I started counting. In one hour, Faolan and I would be going after them. Whether Aidan liked it or not.

gadaíocht an mbeán oíche
A MIDNIGHT HEIST

m o i r a

The city was quiet. Too quiet. It set my nerves on edge. I wished there were people about, chatting and making noise, din that would cover the sound of our feet as we crept behind roundhouses and made wide arcs around jittery horses. But I knew it was technically better this way. The streets were nearly empty, except for a few men stumbling back from the center of town. In the light of the full moon, there was no one around to recognize Louis and Ailill.

Heading toward the mound called Ráth da Dtarbh, we traveled in the shadows. It was cold and the night was clear. It was the kind of early autumn night that would leave a thin layer of frost on the grass in the morning. The hill lay ahead of us, and above, bathed in moonlight. My eyes were on the roundhouse, still some distance away, when I walked right into Louis's outstretched arm.

Ailill was standing flat against the wall of the nearest roundhouse,

inches from the open doorway. When I only stared, Louis grabbed my arm and dragged me to the other side of the door.

"It has to be you," he hissed. "You won't be recognized. Stick your head inside and see how many are in there. If you're spotted, just say you're meeting a certain lad and run away. They'll accept that."

"What is this place?" I asked, but Louis was already creeping away along the wall of the house.

"We'll keep watch," he hissed. Ailill's gaze swung from the top of the road back in the direction we'd come, always on guard.

Light spilled out of the doorway, making a long rectangle on the grass in front of me. *The Girl Marked by the Blood Omen*, I thought darkly. *This could be it for you.*

Shaking my head, I took a deep breath and reminded myself why I was doing this. Why I was taking these risks: my sisters.

I stepped into the light.

The interior of the house was one large, round room, smoky and quiet. There was a ring of beds, and the sound of snores told me more than a few were occupied. But I didn't see anyone stirring. The fire in the middle of the room glinted off something on my right, and I turned sharply.

Weapons. Spears and swords and even a large ax lined the wall to the right of the door. *Aha.* This was what we'd come for. I was just about to duck back out of the door to report my recon to Louis when I realized that would be a waste of time. I glanced around the room one more time. Nobody was awake.

Stepping up to the wall, I found I could reach two spears and lift them off the wall, their heft surprising but manageable. The rest were a little higher. Clutching my two prizes beneath my arm, I stood on my tiptoes and reached. The next nearest weapon was the ax, its blade the size of my head. My fingers couldn't quite get a grip, but I brushed it roughly with my fingertips, trying to knock it off the wall.

It fell loose easily. And clattered against the spears as it fell to the ground.

I froze.

All was silent, except for the shuffling of feet that came from where Louis and Ailill were posted outside. Turning slowly, I surveyed the room. Not a single soul had stirred.

Stooping quietly, I picked up the ax and ran.

"What are you doing, *a leanbh*?" Ailill hissed as I ran up the road away from the roundhouse, stopping only when I needed to catch my breath, the air searing-cold in my lungs.

"This is what we came for, isn't it?" I asked, handing him a spear. Louis was right on his heels, mouth hanging open. I offered him a spear too.

"Did you rob the barracks on your own?" Louis asked, flabbergasted. "Just like that?"

I grinned at him. "Just like that."

"Well, we'll be thanking you to stick to the plan from now on." Ailill shook his head. "And that yoke isn't for you." He plucked the giant ax from my hands and shoved the spear at me. Smiling, I fell into line behind Ailill and Louis as we moved forward toward Ráth da Dtarbh.

Forget about my favorite magic antlers that burned with Bunrowan. I didn't need them to feel powerful anymore. Turned out all you needed to do to feel in control was steal a few ancient weapons right out from under a band of sleeping warriors. Easy.

AS WE stood at the bottom of Ráth da Dtarbh, looking up at the steep staircase to the door, this next bit seemed like a walk in the park. From what Ailill said, this roundhouse was full of young ladies in the queen's court.

"Medb's got visitors at the moment," Ailill whispered as he kneeled in the shadows beside me and Louis. "I've seen the Ulster flag around the place. But for some reason, there's no feastin' happening. Maybe it's over. Or maybe Medb has something planned in the coming days. I know not. But that means everyone inside should be home, but also asleep."

"And if they're not?" I asked, trying not to let the prospect of this plan going awry quash my newfound sense of confidence.

"We don't want trouble," Ailill said. "I can fight if I need to, but these are young'uns in here. First, we try to talk our way out."

"Ailill, you keep watch on the back door," Louis said. "I'll watch the front. It's only girls who live in here, Moira, so you'll have to be the one to scout out the interior."

Ailill looked up at the roundhouse, his impression unreadable. It almost seemed like he was . . . scared of this place. Why would he be scared of a bunch of sleeping kids?

"This time," Louis said, grabbing my arm to pull my attention away from the inscrutable Ailill, "you come straight back. No playing the hero. Get the lay of the land, see if you can spot your sister, and come straight out again. Then we'll do this together."

"Okay," I agreed.

My confidence held up as I followed Louis up the stairs, Ailill bringing up the rear with careful glances in every direction. We'd seen Finbar hanging around, so that meant Bríd was here. I knew it. This side of the hill was shadowed, and we were fast. Ailill slipped around to the back of the house so quietly, I didn't even notice he was gone until the wind whipped around cold and quick in the empty space behind me.

Louis stepped to the side of the door, stood flat against the wall, and nodded at me.

Act natural, I told myself. *Like you live here.*

A door made of vertical planks of wood hinged on a thick, wooden pole, blocking the doorway, but there was no light leaking from beneath it. With luck, everyone here was asleep too.

Ice-cold spear clutched upright in my right hand, I opened the door slowly with my left. When it didn't make a sound, I opened it a little faster. It was very dark, and I slipped inside before the light of the moon woke someone.

Squeezing my spear, I stood for a second, letting my eyes adjust.

The only movement in the one-room house was the fire in the middle of the room, which had died down to embers. Thin trails of smoke swirled up toward the ceiling, escaping through the bright hole that revealed a glimmer of stars beyond.

Directly to my right was a thick, straw pallet holding a girl clutching tightly to a brightly colored woolen blanket. She was curled toward the fire, her blonde hair falling over her cheeks. Most of the room was lined with beds, maybe twelve of them, and each was occupied by a shadow, softly breathing. The only way I would be able to identify Bríd was by getting closer. I studied every shadow from afar—twice—before deciding they were all definitely asleep.

Passing by the blonde girl, I stepped up to the next bed. A figure covered head to toe in a fur-lined blanket was facing the wall, her wide shoulders falling softly with her breath. *No, too tall to be Bríd.* I moved quickly on to the next.

Halfway across the room, I came to an empty bed. My stomach turned. The covers were twisted near the bottom of the pallet, like its occupant had had a nocturnal fight. I touched my palm to the furs covering the straw. They were cold.

Shaking my head and rubbing my hands together for warmth, I moved on. I could speculate about the empty bed later.

The next bed was occupied by a very small girl with light-brown skin. Despite having three beds left to check, I was beginning to panic. Bríd had to be here. Why else would Finbar have been hanging around this place?

"*A Ghardaí!*"

The scream rattled me, and I dropped my spear.

It was the blonde girl by the door screaming her head off like I was a ghost. The whole house was awake in seconds, including the broad-shouldered girl in furs who turned out to be a fully armed guard.

I darted for the door, but even unburdened by my spear, I was no match for the guard. Before I could do much more than gasp, I was standing in front of the fire, my wrists pinched together behind my back.

"Who is she?" the girls whispered to each other.

I was contemplating whether to yell something to Louis or Ailill or keep quiet and hope they got away, when another guard ducked inside the front door. Louis stumbled in beside him, his arms bent behind him too.

No. All the confidence from my stupid weapons heist drained away from me. I kept trying to catch Louis's eye, to communicate somehow, ask how we could alert Ailill. He would come for us. Right? Ailill could take on two guards, surely. He'd been one himself!

Someone threw a log on the fire, and the flames jumped toward the ceiling, throwing us into light.

"The *ollam*?" one of the girls cried. The whispering grew in volume as the girls stood on tiptoe to get a good look at Louis, their disgraced bard. And then the most horrible noise of all reached my ears: the sound of metal on metal coming from the back door. Someone was fighting Ailill.

No. Ailill was our last hope. How would we ever communicate with Ríona and Aidan back in the cave? Still, Louis avoided my eyes.

"Why have you come back?" The blonde girl who'd raised the alarm stepped forward, her arms crossed over her chest. She shivered in the cold, but her fierce blue eyes flashed as she stared Louis down.

Louid only looked at the ground, a miserable defeat on his face.

"Who are you with, *Ollam*?" the girl, who appeared to be in charge here, demanded.

Just then, Ailill stumbled through the back door, his arms bound with rope. His guard looked a little worse for the wear, but triumphant nonetheless.

No, no, no. God, no.

We had failed. How had we *failed*?

Staring at Ailill, the blonde girl looked as if she'd seen yet another ghost, this one more terrifying than the first. "*A Dhaid*?" she cried, her blue eyes round and flashing in the light of the fire.

Dad? Did that make this girl . . . Medb's daughter?

"Fenora," Ailill said, defeat thick in his voice. He was hunched and breathing heavily, two bruises blooming on his left cheek.

The guard holding Louis let out a startling laugh, deep and broken, and pointed at Ailill. "Welcome back, *mo Rí*." *My king*.

"What's going on here?" the girl called Fenora demanded, but her voice shook. Her gaze flew back and forth between me and Louis and her father.

"This one of them Morrigan girls?" the guard holding my hands asked one of his mates. "The queen thought the *ollam* would be sniffing around people more powerful than him, didn't she?"

"Might be." His friend shrugged, cocking his head at me. "Didn't bet on every inch of this city being guarded, did ya? You can thank your sister for that."

"My sister?" I gasped. So, she was here. Somewhere.

"Enough shite talk," the last guard said, pushing Ailill toward the front door.

"Remind me again how you wanted to talk yourself out of this one, Ailill?" Louis muttered. His guard shook him violently and turned him toward the door.

Fenora's eyes flew between her father and the guards. I couldn't tell whether she wanted to spare him or let them do their duty. It didn't matter. The guards knew their orders implicitly.

The one holding me fast shoved me after the others. "Ye lot go straight to Medb."

geata go hifreann
THE GATE TO HELL

bríd

The cell was just as I had left it. I stood near the back, on one leg, the other tucked up under me, with one eye open. What had I done? Of all the stupid feckin' things I'd done in my life . . .

Unbeknownst to me, I'd been playing Medb's little game this entire time. She'd known what I'd been planning, or at least that I was planning something. The kitchen maids had reported to their queen exactly what happened in the kitchens that night, or maybe she simply found Finbar missing and realized where my thoughts would go. It didn't matter. Either way, she had known, then, that I would make an attempt. An attempt at something rash. Of course, I'd done exactly that, just before stumbling right into her rooms, reeking of guilt. And probably bog rosemary.

Then she'd used my pigheadedness to not only lock me up again but to get exactly what she'd wanted from Fenora.

Fenora. I pressed the heels of my palms against my eyelids. Something sour in my soul told me trusting Fenora had been a mistake from the start. After finally discovering Finbar and Dad, I'd found it so easy to believe Fenora was as evil as her mother. After all, I'd introduced Fenora to Finbar, and then he'd disappeared. Had she learned exactly what would hurt me, what could be used against me, and acted on it? Had she given up my heart, my soul, put my crow right in the hands of her queen? But then she'd made a deal with Medb to spare my life. She'd made that comment, about me being their only way of attracting the Morrigu . . . that indicated she didn't know Medb even had my dad. And then she'd given up her entire future. For me.

Of course, that could all have been part of the game. Part of this game I'd been playing in Medb's court. A game I'd lost by murdering someone in cold blood and earning myself a place back in this dank cave beneath Ráth Cruachan. *You deserve this,* I thought miserably.

I'd also earned two guards posted just outside. They walked back and forth, chatting to each other and spitting in the dirt and throwing glances my way every so often. I was caught and on display, like a feckin' goldfish. At least now that it was dark, they couldn't stare. Pulling the thin, scratchy blanket around me, I sat on the hay pallet and stared at the guards' backs.

To my surprise, they were speaking in hushed tones to a third person.

The guards exchanged a look and then slowly stepped aside. The door to the cell opened, and a figure stepped into the gloom. She removed her hood, and the moonlight hit her golden hair.

"No." Scrambling to my feet, I cut her off in the middle of the room. "You can't be here."

You can't be here because you're either a traitor or too good for me. Either way, I needed her to leave. Her being here was hurting me, whipping my insides into a fury.

"It's fine," Fenora said. "I promised them—"

"No!" I interrupted, wind lashing my veins. "You can't be here because I don't want you here."

Fenora stepped back, as if I'd slapped her. "I saved your life," she said softly. "I-I sacrificed . . . everything."

"Does that sacrifice make up for all the lying and the kidnapping?" I was goading her, I knew it. Deep down, I wanted to make her so mad that she'd scream her innocence. That she'd convince me, once and for all, that she wasn't in league with her mother. Because otherwise, I wasn't sure if I could ever fully believe her.

Fenora's eyes, blue as the sea, went watery. "I-I never lied to you."

That wasn't a resounding defense. "But the kidnapping you won't deny? Is that what you did to Finbar? After I introduced you to him, you took him to your mother?"

Fenora's mouth fell open just the slightest bit. "You believe that?"

"What else am I to believe? And what about my father? Did you know where he was this whole time?"

Fenora gaped at me. Then she pressed her lips together, resigned. "So he's here."

My heart stuttered. Was her surprise genuine?

The look on my face must have been somewhere between confusion and disbelief, because Fenora looked at me and her mouth turned down. Her eyes filled with water. "And you believe me capable of all that?"

"The daughter of Medb?" I said, with a little shrug. I'd put on my thick armor of confidence and flippancy, but inside, I didn't know what to believe. My heart was being tugged in all different directions, but the cadence of our conversation was rolling too fast to stop it. The exchange was building with too much unspoken.

"Of course," Fenora whispered. "I'm the daughter of Medb. Why wouldn't I strike down everything in her way?"

She turned to go, but stopped near the door. "Úna will live," she said softly. "If you care to know."

Her sarcasm hit me deep. I opened my mouth for some scathing reply in this distrustful tug-of-war we were locked in, but Fenora interrupted me.

"There's one more thing you should know." She forced a smile onto her face and looked me in the eye. "She's building an army. My mother. At least, that's her plan. I don't know how she intends to do it, but if I believed anyone capable of it, it would be Medb of Connacht."

Was that meant to intimidate me? "That doesn't scare me," I spat. "You and your mother don't scare me." I was terrified.

Fenora shook her head, her lips parted in disbelief. The guards appeared at the door, perhaps sensing the tension, ready to protect their princess. But Fenora raised her hand to them. "One more moment."

They exchanged an uneasy look and stepped away again.

"There's a cave," Fenora told me. "On the edge of Cruachan. On the other side—your side. They say the Morrigan can call creatures forth from the Gate to Hell."

The wind whipped up, and I suddenly felt short of breath, as if all the air inside me were forming a tornado in my chest.

"Dangerous creatures," Fenora whispered. "Things that will do the Morrigan's bidding."

My arms were shaking. I was losing control of my arms and legs and even my tongue felt out of my command. This was it. The gale tossing inside me told me this was it. No matter what had happened between us before, Fenora wasn't lying now. This was how we had to kill Medb.

"Medb may build an army, yes, but the Morrigan has a power far greater than that," Fenora said softly. Her tears had stopped, but the watery blue of her eyes seemed unsteady. Stepping through the door, she twisted her lips to one side and whispered, "We were never meant to trust each other. Goodbye, Bríd."

She turned away, just as I felt the soles of my feet lift off the ground. What little control I'd had over my limbs was outmatched. I floated there, arms outstretched like wings, toes barely scraping the straw on the floor as the guards shut the door after Fenora, their eyes on the ground, and turned away from me.

This was it. This wouldn't be over while Medb was alive. And to beat her, we had to go to the Gate to Hell.

eitilt san oíche

NIGHT FLIGHT

bríd

I didn't mean to fall asleep. But everything happening inside me, the magic that made me levitate and see the future, it was too powerful. It exhausted me. Remembering the explosion that I'd unleashed in the kitchens when I'd found Finbar, I'd tried to do the same to the bars of my cell. To no avail. Nothing had happened, but the effort had shaken me to my core, and my limbs had been too heavy for my body. One moment, I'd been sitting down on the bed to consider my next move, and the next I was asleep.

Or rather, I was flying over Cruachan. It was strange, the moment I realized I was asleep but feeling the air so cold on my skin. Shivers raced down my spine. The wind was freezing as I swooped around the mounds like a bird. Like my arms were wings. I tried to look at my arms, but I couldn't see anything except the twinkling stars above and the soft lights of the town below.

Finbar was there too. Not really there. But I could feel him there. As if he were with me in spirit.

Looping around Ráth Cruachan, I headed north. Nothing told me where to go; I just knew. Dream me knew. And right as I lifted my gaze to see where I was going, Cruachan disappeared. It had been there one moment, gone the next.

And a giant hawthorn tree loomed in front of me. I was so surprised by Cruachan's disappearance, I had to swerve to miss the tree, and that was when I saw it—a tiny gap in the earth. The entrance to a cave.

This had to be it. My body knew it, even when my mind didn't understand. This was the Gate to Hell.

Light as a bird, I flew into the gap and was greeted by a snarling dog. *Conry!* He was climbing to his feet in the dark cave, edging forward but still giving me a wide berth. Sensing I was meant to fly down the rocky tunnel he guarded, I swooped above his head and continued.

Not far ahead, I saw a figure curled on the floor, snoring. Another paced near the far end of the tunnel, a wolf at her heels. The human turned, and her eyes went wide.

Ríona!

"Finbar!" she signed with unsteady fingers.

Ríona was here, in Cruachan. And she had found the Gate to Hell before me. Where was Moira? I flew around, searching, but the figure on the floor was too thick to be Moira. I tried to tamp down my worry. Ríona was here, at the very place we needed to be, so they must have learned things I didn't know yet. Shaky excitement flooded me, and I felt like my heart might burst, knock me right out of the air.

Was this real? Was this a premonition? Could I show Ríona how to come find me? Flapping excitedly, I tossed my tiny body around her head and then swooped toward the cave entrance.

Follow me, Ríona!

She bent to wake the sleeping figure, and Aidan's sleepy face gazed up at me. She was tugging on his arm, trying to follow me. *Yes! Yes!*

There was a growl from behind me, and I blinked, startled.

When I opened my eyes, I was in my cell beneath Ráth Cruachan. My body fell to the bed with a *thump*. My breathing was fast, too fast. I couldn't get enough air into my lungs as I clutched at the bed, the things around me, to convince myself it was true—I was awake again.

Had any of that been real? If it had ... My heart was beating painfully fast as I realized Ríona coming here would be exactly what Medb wanted. It would be playing right into Medb's plans. *Again. Bríd, you eejit!* I never should have lured Ríona to come find me.

My only hope was that she couldn't. That she didn't find Cruachan. *Abeg, please, don't let Ríona find this place.*

The same fatigue from earlier was battering my senses, my heart racing, my eyes welling with tears. It was as if my magic cost me in energy, in breaths, in consciousness. I was thinking desperately of Ríona, and Moira, and the Gate to Hell when everything went dark.

rúin uladh

SECRETS OF ULSTER

m o i r a

The guards steered us none too gently into a long, wooden hall with a high ceiling. Louis grunted and spat and cursed and generally put up a fight as his guard tried to get him through the door. I didn't see the point. Neither, it seemed, did Ailill.

He looked broken, defeated. Guilt lanced through my heart. I had brought him here. I had made him come. And now he was going to be back at the mercy of the woman he had loved . . . who had tried to kill him.

At the end of the hall was a throne of fire. It was made of wood, carved from an array of oranges and reds, to resemble flames crawling up the wall. A window in the back wall of the hall threw the light of the moon onto the throne, and it gleamed like the flames would jump to life any moment.

As I studied it, a woman stepped in front of it and sat. Her smile

was imperious, her pale white skin glowing in the light of the moon. Her dark hair fell long and wild over her shoulders. And at her forehead rested a thin glimmering crown.

So this was the Queen Medb.

She sat, smiling, as we approached. Louis's struggle and our shuffling footsteps were the only sounds. Several people appeared behind and on either side of the throne, whispering and glancing at Medb. Advisors, maybe. Or more guards. While I watched, Ailill's daughter, Fenora, stepped out of the assembled crowd to stand beside her mother.

When the guards tugged us to a standstill directly before the throne, Medb stood and closed the distance between us. I was her first target.

"Macha," she said. Her voice was firm, commanding. But also oddly . . . emotionless.

Everything in me went cold. *Macha.* She'd said it so easily, like she'd known me all my life, by no other name. *Macha, a goddess of the land. With healing powers.* That's what the old woman on Inis Mór had told Ríona.

"How wonderful." Medb shook her head, as if in disbelief. She looked back at Fenora, who merely pressed her lips together. "And how did you come to be here, hm?" Medb asked me. "Who brought you to our fair city?" She clasped her hands at her waist and turned to look at Louis. "You, I was expecting," she said. "You were part of the plan. But you . . ." She turned, walked to stand in front of Ailill, and placed a long finger under his chin, tipping his head up. "You are unexpected."

"You always used to like that about me," Ailill muttered, his eyes on the floor.

The guards shifted uncomfortably, and the people around the room muttered to each other. I braced myself for Medb's wrath. But she only smiled.

"Too right," she said, shaking her head. "You may not have been the first to share my crown, or even the second. But I loved you longest." With a curl of her nail, she released Ailill's chin. "Still, things change, *mo chuisle*."

"That I know too well," Ailill said, and for the first time, he lifted his gaze to Medb's. They looked at each other for a moment that felt far too private for the rest of us to be watching. After several moments, Medb took a deep breath and turned back to Louis.

His gaze freed, Ailill looked desperately at his daughter. The girl looked away.

"And you, my dear Cú Chulainn," Medb said, shaking her head. "We have more history than anyone, do we not?"

Louis had finally stopped struggling with his guard, but his shoulders were squared to his former queen. He looked at her with his head cocked back, chin raised.

"I must say, I applaud you," Medb said, walking back to her throne and sitting, as though we were enjoying a pleasant chat in the park. "Using Ailill mac Máta to get around the triskele oath. Very well done."

"I had little choice after narrowly escaping your assassin," Louis spat.

Medb nodded slowly. "Oh, don't take that personally, Cú Chulainn. You know as well as I do that your tally of murder attempts far outnumbers mine."

"Maybe, but your tally of successes is greater than mine," he said. "Do you remember Dundalk? Conspiring to lure the great Cú Chulainn to his death? My most painful death, by far."

"Yet," Medb said. Your most painful death *yet*."

God, my head was spinning. I felt like I was listening to someone read one of Ríona's storybooks out loud. Of course, Ailill had told us Louis's story, who he was—*Lú, god of sun and storms; the great Cú Chulainn; Louis, ollam of Cruachan.* But to hear him speak so freely about his past was quite another thing altogether. He had a history with Queen Medb. A bloody one.

"My, you do hold a grudge," Medb said, shaking her head. "I'd thought we'd put all that behind us. We made you our *ollam*. You served us justly."

"And, in return, you told me you were seeking the Morrigan to give her back her rightful place at the head of Ireland, to take Connacht, and then, eventually, reform the Ériu of old." Louis pulled his arms forward, trying to escape his guard. "That was a lie, wasn't it? You intend to usurp her power instead. To rule as much of Ireland as you can."

Medb watched the guard wrangle him back into control. Fenora's eyes kept flicking between her mother and her father.

"Tell me," Medb said calmly, "what exactly did you think rebuilding the Ériu of old would entail?"

A bitter feeling rose in my stomach. *Louis, how could you be so naive?* He'd believed in her, in this place and what Medb wanted to achieve, right up until she'd turned on him. Until she'd sent her henchman to finish him.

"It won't work!" Louis yelled. "Your pathetic city here at Cruachan, it will get nowhere out there. It's a whole different world. You wish to retake Connacht? Just try it. The rest of Ireland will come for you. And then the ways of old will really and truly be dead." He was free for a split second, stalking toward the throne, before the guard regained control of him.

Medb stood and walked to the scuffling pair, stopping uncomfortably close to Louis. He flinched back, chest heaving. Medb whispered something I couldn't hear, reaching out to touch her palm to Louis's arm. I thought they were having a private conversation—but then Louis touched his forearm, and I saw what she'd done. The triskele mark had faded until it looked like nothing more than an old tattoo.

"Oath magic," Medb said, sighing. "I never should have relied upon so old a thing." She brushed her hands together as if to rid them of dirt and looked Louis in the face. "Of course, it suited me in the end. When plans changed and I needed you to help the Morrigan get here. Well ..." She motioned toward me as evidence that her plan had worked. "Let us deal in truths, shall we? That is what you want?"

"You don't know the meaning of the word," Louis said, deadly venom in his voice. If ever I had questioned his intentions—which I had, right up until this moment—I never would again.

"Those who wield the truth as a weapon must know it more intimately than anyone," Medb said, her smile back. "Tell me, exactly what truth would you like to know?"

"Why is Ulster here?" Ailill asked before Louis could say anything.

Medb sighed, as if she were growing tired of this conversation and would act soon. Only, I had no idea what she was going to do. What would she do with us? With Ailill? With Louis? With me? Was this how the Blood Omen would be fulfilled?

"Yes, there is a party from Ulster staying with us in Cruachan at this moment." People watched eagerly from around the room, and I wondered if any of them were the visitors. "They were sent, on my invitation, by Conchobar."

Fenora's head snapped up, Louis gaped, and Ailill shook his head slowly, his mouth open. Whispering broke out among the spectators. Their astonishment made my heart race. What did this mean? Who was Conchobar?

"You are surprised?" Medb asked, clearly pretending not to enjoy their confusion.

Louis scoffed, jerking his arms forward again. But the guard had learned his lesson. He held Louis fast. "The only man who can claim a bloodier history than my own with the Queen of Connacht is Conchobar mac Nessa." Louis strained against his guard, his face going red. "I can only hope that he's lured you into this pact to kill you."

Ailill was as still as a statue, even as the people began to shift nervously around us. I wondered if he had a surefire plan to get us out of here—or if he'd just given up. "What business have you with your first husband?" Ailill asked calmly.

First husband?

"There's no need for jealousy," Medb said slyly. "It's purely business. Because Cú Chulainn is right. Connacht couldn't take the island alone. But Connacht and Ulster? Conchobar holds the key to Ulster, and so I need him. Together, we'll use the power of the

Morrigan to solidify our reign and take all of Ireland."

Ailill and Louis looked at each other over my head, and the fear in their eyes was chilling. Beside the throne, Medb's daughter was going pale. A few spectators had escaped to the door, while others stared, rapt.

"No!" I screamed.

Medb's eyes landed on me. She raised one brow in amusement. "Macha objects."

How I wished I had the magical antlers now, to feel some modicum of control. "You'll never get my sister," I shouted at her, yanking my arms free. The guard shoved me to the floor, and I landed hard on my knees, my arms imprisoned again almost instantly. Beside me, Louis roared and pulled away from his guard. The man was on him again in seconds.

"You think not?" Medb asked me, ignoring the tussle. "What about your other sister? Would you like to see her now? It will make for quite the family reunion."

The need to see Bríd, to see that she was all right, filled me with anger.

"I now have two of the sisters three." Medb raised her arms. "Tell me, how do I complete my collection?"

This woman before me had torn my family apart. Now, I wanted to tear *her* apart.

"You will *never* get her," I screamed, and as I tried to rip my arms free, the scream continued. On and on, a primal sound I didn't know I could make. Louis was still shouting, and Ailill looked on, helpless. I screamed for every moment I had not been here to protect Bríd and every moment I would not be there to save Ríona.

The doors to the great hall slammed open.

A buzzing filled the air, and a massive swarm of bees leaked into the hall from the darkness outside. Suddenly, there were bats among them, swooping under the threshold, and then birds with wings as black as Finbar's making a raucous fit to wake the dead. Next, the air went dark with insects, their hissing intermingling with the twitters of mice that skittered over the floor so thickly you couldn't see the stone.

The spectators around the room screamed. Medb stared, aghast. Looking back and forth between her and Ailill and Louis, I began to shake. If this wasn't Medb's doing . . .

I stumbled to my feet, and my captor let me, distracted as he was by the horror swarming near the door. Bees, bats, insects I couldn't name—the air was thick with them. Five large deer entered the hall, giant racks of antlers swaying with each step.

And then Ríona stepped through the doorway, her arms outstretched, her beautiful hair flying in every direction, as though each strand were electrified.

an bhuile

THE FRENZY

ríona

"No!" Moira screamed. "Ríona, run!"

I walked steadily forward, my chin tipped up in the air, my eyes on Medb. Faolan walked at my side, his fur on end, his teeth bared, his yellow eyes glistening. Above him, Finbar swooped around and around my head. And on my other side, Conry. Louis's hound stared at Medb with the practiced stare of a hunter.

And the creatures . . . the wild creatures. They moved along with me, matching my pace, moving steadily toward my target.

"Get her!" Medb screamed at her guards. "Get the Morrigu!"

At once, the guards holding Moira, Ailill, and Louis dropped their captives and dashed toward me. Spears and swords appeared out of nowhere, someone behind the throne tossing them to anyone who could catch. Most of the spectators were fleeing through a door at the back of the hall, and Medb simply stood there, staring at me with wide

eyes.

The truth came to me, blooming into existence in my mind: *we are more powerful than she expected.*

Behind me, Bó *harrumphed* as he stepped into the hall, Aidan on his back. Moira stared at the pair longingly before shaking herself and grabbing on to the spear of a passing guard. Surprised, he nearly tripped, and Moira yanked. He went sprawling, and she dashed away.

Meanwhile, Louis had broken free from his own captor, and Ailill was running toward a blonde girl standing beside the throne.

"Faigh í!" Medb screamed. "Get her, you fools."

Taking a deep breath, I slowly began to raise my arms. I did it just like I had on the edge of Cruachan, where magic had tingled along my arms as Finbar had led us into a city that shouldn't have existed. There, between our world and this, I'd lifted my arms and concentrated on the wild energy coursing through my veins, that feeling of something about to happen that I associated with the curios. Slowly, like I'd been gently pulling out a splinter, I'd nudged at that energy, that feeling, that *frenzy.* I hadn't even seen all the animals that had answered my call yet because there had been too many.

It felt like an eternity, but the moment my fingertips pointed to the ceiling of Medb's court, chaos rained down upon her guards.

Men screamed as the bees swarmed. The deer ran, head down, into the throng, scattering most and goring the rest. The mice climbed the men's legs, drawing blood, and I flicked my left hand to take them in a wide circle around Moira. I breathed deeply; my nostrils flared. Eyes darting right, I spotted a guard who had gained too much ground and flicked my right wrist to break three sparrow hawks away from the flock. They began a bloody assault on their target with the squawking of an animal five times their size.

It wasn't until Bó reared up, lethal hooves striking a man's chest, sending him flying across the room, that I realized how close I'd come to being grabbed by his meaty fists. They wouldn't injure me; I knew that. Medb needed me. Well, it would take more than one of her guards to take me alive.

"Moira, get back!" Aidan yelled, nodding toward the door, and I saw Moira just a few steps away, stumbling this way and that, unsure what to do.

Using my left hand to guide the bees to open patches of skin on the nearest guard, I looked at her and signed just one letter: *"B."*

Gulping, Moira nodded. She turned around, stopped, and then turned the other way, indecisive. And then someone grabbed her arm.

I nearly whipped the bees onto the girl's face, but Moira held up a hand to stop me. The blonde girl looked between us. "I know where she is," she said breathlessly.

A few feet away from us, Ailill had stepped in front of me and was taking on two guards and besting them easily. Aidan and Bó worked the right flank, keeping the guards in a tight knot that didn't give them room to properly use their weapons. I needed to focus.

"Bríd," the girl said, her blue eyes round. "I can take you to her."

Moira bit her lip.

"Go!" I signed at her before whipping back around and digging deep inside myself. In this moment, I didn't feel anyone else's emotions. There were no outside thoughts scrabbling at my brain. No, in this moment, it was just me and that feeling inside me drowning out everything else. Just me and the Frenzy.

seasamh an rí
THE KING'S STAND

b r í d

The noise from the hall was growing louder. What was happening? I'd regained consciousness to find only one guard outside my cell door, the others streaming toward Medb's throne room.

"What's going on?" I asked the remaining guard, stepping up behind him and threading my hands through the bars.

He jumped, looking at me and then quickly away. "Go back to sleep. It's none of your concern."

He spotted Fenora tearing down the path at the same moment I did. Only, I recognized the girl on her heels. *Moira!*

The guard stepped uneasily away from the cell, but he wasn't on the defensive yet. He knew and trusted Fenora. He hadn't even drawn his sword when Fenora grabbed the spear from Moira's arms and whipped it against his head.

He fell like a pile of rocks, the thump drowned out by the wild

sounds emanating from above.

"Moira!" I gasped. "What the feck is happening?"

"We're getting you out of here; that's what's happening," Moira hissed.

Fenora clawed at the guard's clothes and finally came away with a key. The minute the cell door opened, I launched myself into Moira's arms.

"You're okay," she cried, squeezing me tightly.

"*You're* okay," I cried back. My eyes fell on Fenora. I released Moira and looked at Fenora, fighting to keep my voice steady. "Thank you," I said softly. "Thank you for bringing my sister to me."

"We can't dawdle," Moira said, tugging on my arm. "We have to get back to Ríona. You should see her, Bríd. She's doing it; she's really doing it."

"Wait," I grabbed her arm, stopping her in her tracks. "Dad is here. We have to get Dad." Without stopping to explain, I darted toward the cell where Dad was kept.

"Bríd," Fenora called after me.

She reached me, panting, at the same moment that I saw for myself what she wanted to tell me: "He's not here."

"Where is he?" I demanded, rounding on her.

Her big blue eyes closed. "I don't know." She shook her head and looked me in the eye. "I swear I don't know. After you told me he was here, I went looking for him. But I couldn't find him."

She'd gone looking for Dad. When I'd told her he was here, she'd believed me. After I hadn't believed her.

Behind us, the desperate sound of animals broke into the night air.

We whirled around. Ríona, in a moving, undulating, screeching, squawking swarm of wild animals, was making her way down the stairs of Ráth Cruachan.

"What the f—"

"There's no time, Bríd!" Moira yelled, grabbing my arm and running to meet Ríona at the bottom of the stairs. Aidan was already in the street, riding Bó, fending off a handful of guards who'd been approaching from a side street.

"Bríd!" Moira shouted, gesturing for me to follow. Finbar swooped around my head with a happy squawk before reporting right back to Ríona. She was at the bottom of the stairs now, attacking any guard who wandered too close, dousing them with mice and bats and bees. Faolan was at her side, a whirl of claws and teeth, and even Moira helped, pelting approaching guards with rocks. Louis and a great, big, burly man stood halfway up the stairs, shoving away any guard who made a run for the Morrigu, while Conry chased them away, snarling.

Fenora was at my side.

"Who is that?" I asked her of the man who fought for us.

"Ailill mac Mata. The last king of Connacht," she said softly. "My father."

"*Oya*, Bríd, let's go!" Moira screamed. She was shoving people out of the way, clearing a path for Ríona. I had so many questions to ask Fenora, and I longed to look into her eyes, to see how she was, but my sisters needed help. Springing into action, I elbowed my way into the melee, grabbed a rock off the ground, and threw it as hard as I could at a man barreling toward us. That's when I saw a man with a sword coming for Louis.

"Louis!" I screamed.

He ducked the well-placed swing at the last possible second. Fenora's father stepped forward to bring the offender to the ground. The guard scrabbled backward, trying to escape Ailill's grasp. I saw Ailill's gaze dart once to Ráth Cruachan.

At the top of the stairs, limned in the light of her great hall, her dark red dress a gash against the night, stood Medb. Her cold gaze missed nothing. And Fenora, her mother's frown on her face, stood alone in the street, watching her father fight her mother's men. She looked cold. She looked lost. She looked like every dream she'd ever had of vegetable gardens and animals to love her had evaporated.

"Get out!" Ailill shouted at Ríona and Louis, gesturing down an empty street. "I can hold them, but you lot have to get out before the whole city is upon us. They won't cross the barrier tonight. They're not ready."

Ríona and Louis were a team, each covering the other's back, a rotating funnel of danger. Conry, Faolan, and Finbar circled them, focused only on their protection. Moira was beside Bó now, Aidan reaching down to swing her up onto the True Mare's back. Everyone was accounted for. Well, almost everyone . . .

"Fenora!" I shouted. Her eyes, confused at first, found mine. She stumbled toward me. "Come with us."

A smile slowly grew on her face, and she looked at me like I'd finally said something she'd been waiting to hear. She grabbed my hand. Closing her eyes, she sighed, her shoulders falling with the motion. And then, with one shake of her head, she broke my heart in two.

She leaned forward and kissed me, her lips feather-soft and warm. The warmth spread to my chest, lifting my heart until I felt my feet grow light on the ground. Another moment, and I'd be floating. Fenora dropped my hand and backed away. My feet were heavy in the dirt once again.

"Fenora!" I pleaded. But she only shook her head at me, tears welling in her eyes.

Before I could say anything more, Louis had my arm in his hand, and I was tripping after him, Conry nudging the backs of my legs. Ríona came behind us, her horde keeping anyone who followed us at bay. Finbar swooped down to fly circles around me, but I kept glancing over my shoulder.

Fenora had disappeared from my sight. Ailill was in the street now, guards pouring down the steps from the great hall and appearing from the opposite street, where the barracks were. We were nearly at a turn in the street that I knew would take us right to the ditch that encircled Cruachan. Once we were beyond that . . .

I looked back once more. Ailill stood, his hands at his sides, surrounded. An ax glinted high above them all and came down too quick to see.

Fenora's scream tore through me. Louis's hands were on me, dragging me backward, toward the ditch, toward the world outside Cruachan.

Bó reared around. "What was that?" Moira demanded.

"It was Ailill," Louis said, determination on his face as he marched forward. Moira nodded once, and they rode on to the very edge of the ditch. Bó stood, one leg raised, as if she knew what to do. Which, I realized, she did. She'd gotten here somehow, hadn't she?

Ríona's eyes glistened as she turned to face us, each of us standing at the edge of the trench. Only a handful of guards still trailed us, kept at a distance by Ríona's horde. The deer took one guard down as I watched. Ríona looked from Moira to Aidan. And then to Louis. Her gaze lingered there. He assessed the guards and then smiled at Ríona, nodding.

Last, Ríona looked at me. Without warning, she dropped her arms to her sides, and all the creatures around us scattered. The deer cantered across the trench and disappeared beyond it. The mice disappeared into dark corners, and the insects dissipated. The birds took to the sky, and the bees swarmed back toward Ráth Cruachan, disappearing behind the hall.

She used Medb's own bees against her. "The divine feminine," I whispered.

The remaining guards were injured and in shock. They cowered away from us.

With a nod toward Louis, Ríona stepped forward. There was a shove at my back, somebody was whispering, and I fell onto my stomach. I scrambled back up onto scratched knees and turned frantically in the dust, only to confirm what I knew would be true.

Cruachan was gone.

an tseirbheáil
THE SUMMONING

l o u i s

She looked feral as she stood before the gaping black hole at the end of the tunnel. What had Medb told her while she'd been imprisoned there? All the others watched Bríd warily too. Like she was a wild animal that had just been let out of her cage. The gold stitching in the green dress she wore glowed in the light of the sunrise, which was just beginning to turn the sky pink. It was clearly a dress she'd been given in Cruachan.

Ríona stepped forward and touched her sister's shoulder.

"Bríd, are you okay?" Moira asked. She and Aidan were wrapped in each other's arms in the corner of the cave. Aidan had some scratches and a rather ugly red gash across his left cheek, but Moira had been too afraid to use her healing powers since the incident on the boat. Instead, she was dabbing at his wound with a piece of cloth she'd dipped in the stream outside.

"I know what we have to do."

We all looked at Bríd. Moira and Ríona shrugged at each other.

"To rescue Dad?" Moira asked gently.

Bríd shook her head. "To destroy Medb." Bríd still stood staring into the darkness, far closer to the end of the tunnel than Ailill had allowed any of us before.

"How do you know?" Moira asked.

"Fenora told me. Medb's daughter." Bríd's shoulders rose and fell sharply. Nobody had discussed it yet, but I gathered that something had happened between Bríd and Fenora. Of course, I knew Fenora, a quiet, secretive child who'd grown up with disdain for Cruachan and everything in it. For good reason. When you're the daughter of Medb, your future is nothing but a strategic move in a never-ending bid for power.

Silence fell over us as we felt the weight of Ailill's absence and Bríd felt . . . whatever she'd experienced in Cruachan. Ailill would be dead by now. I was sure of it. Medb wouldn't let him live after all he'd done. The immortality he'd bought over centuries of his life would be easily taken by someone with Medb's knowledge. She had helped him get it. She would be able to take it away.

"OK." Crossing her arms over her chest, Moira stood. "What is it that we have to do? In order to rescue Dad. And stop Medb."

Bríd finally turned to face us. She looked like a Cruachan girl, her dark hair in short braids, her dress rumpled and speckled with dirt. The girls of Cruachan were a force unto themselves. Bríd had been changed by the experience. I hoped her sisters understood that.

"We have to open the Gate to Hell."

acknowledgments

Every time I finish a story, I realize again just how many people contribute to the final book. Here are just a few . . .

Big and eternal thanks to Amy, who whips my sad, weak little manuscripts into shape each and every time.

To my friend Rebecca, my Irish translator for this series, for all her love of the Irish language, and for having me out to her gorgeous home on Inis Oírr. Oh, and her tiny Sonaí for showing me around the place!

Thank you to Renee for her deep and thoughtful reading of this series. Every comment of hers makes my characters stronger and my stories better. Any ignorant slipups are my own, but you can bet Ríona's a badass thanks in big part to Renee.

Thanks, Sara, for your keen eye, sure, but also for just generally being kind and really hilarious.

And to Lyssa, for laying my stories out beautifully, and for all the hard work you do for Snowy Wings Publishing. I'm so grateful for all my fellow Snowy Wings authors, and the awesome Snow Angels, who ceaselessly lend their magic to these dreams of ours.

Props to my mom and dad for always being my first readers, and for putting up with me for the last three decades. And for teaching me that reading and writing books is one of life's ultimate pleasures.

And last, of course, to my own Irishman, Michael, and our sweet furbaby, Lucy, who make the day-to-day of life a pleasure.

A short, dog-obsessed, ketchup-loving romantic from the middle of the U.S., Annie Cosby spent three years living in Galway, Ireland, which gave her mono, set her soul on fire, and introduced her to her husband.

She is the author of the *USA Today*-recommended *Hearts Out of Water* series and lives in St. Louis, Missouri, with a Rottweiler mix named Lucy and her favorite Irishman.

Sign up for her Readers Club and find more bookish fun at AnnieCosby.com.

books by annie cosby

HEARTS OUT OF WATER

All the Tales We Tell

Lifespan of a Memory

The Last Secret

Fadó, Fadó: Selkies, Kelpies and Other Celtic Creatures

(A Companion Collection to Hearts Out of Water)

SOULS OUT OF IRELAND

The Daughters of Morrigan

The Court of Medb